True love! nice s

P9-ECL-253

"We were getting along so well. What did I do to spoil the mood?"

"Nothing," Dorian answered.

Raif had always been perceptive where she was concerned. "You thought I intended to kiss you," he said gently.

"Well, I . . . yes," she admitted.

"Would that be so terrible?"

She moistened her lips. "It wouldn't be a good idea."

"I think it would be a fantastic idea."

For one wild moment, Dorian agreed with him. Then, aware of her own vulnerability, she summoned every ounce of willpower she had. If Raif kissed her, it wouldn't end there. Not when they both wanted the same thing. . . .

Dear Reader,

Welcome to **Silhouette Special Edition** . . . welcome to
romance. Each month, **Silhouette Special Edition**
publishes six novels with you in mind—stories of love
and life, tales that you can identify with—romance
with that little "something special" added in.

This month, **Silhouette Special Edition** has some
wonderful stories on their way to you. A "delivery"
you may want to keep an eye out for is *Navy Baby,* by
Debbie Macomber. It's full steam ahead for a
delightful story that shouldn't be missed!

Rounding out October are winning tales by more of
your favorite authors: Tracy Sinclair, Natalie Bishop,
Mary Curtis, Christine Rimmer and Diana Whitney.
A good time will be had by all!

In each **Silhouette Special Edition** novel, we're
dedicated to bringing you the romances that you
dream about—the type of stories that delight as well
as bring a tear to the eye. And that's what **Silhouette
Special Edition** is all about—special books by special
authors for special readers!

I hope you enjoy this book and all of the stories
to come.

Sincerely,

Tara Gavin
Senior Editor

TRACY SINCLAIR
The Man She Married

Silhouette Special Edition

Published by Silhouette Books New York

America's Publisher of Contemporary Romance

SILHOUETTE BOOKS
300 East 42nd St., New York, N.Y. 10017

THE MAN SHE MARRIED

ISBN: 0-373-09701-8

First Silhouette Books printing October 1991

Printed in the U.S.A.

Books by Tracy Sinclair

TRACY SINCLAIR,

author of more than thirty Silhouette novels, also contributes to various magazines and newspapers. She says her years as a photojournalist provided the most exciting adventures and misadventures of her life. An extensive traveler—from Alaska to South America, and most places in between—and a dedicated volunteer worker, this California resident has accumulated countless fascinating experiences, settings and acquaintances to draw on in plotting her romances.

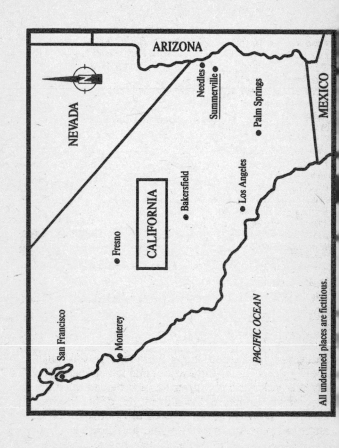

ARIZONA

NEVADA

Needles

Summerville

Palm Springs

CALIFORNIA

Bakersfield

Los Angeles

Fresno

MEXICO

San Francisco

Monterey

PACIFIC OCEAN

All underlined places are fictitious.

Chapter One

The weathered sign on the outskirts of town read Summerville Pop. 24,673. The population had grown since the sign was erected, but Summerville was still a small California town near the Nevada border.

Dorian Merrill should have returned months before to dispose of her parents' possessions and sell their house, but she'd kept finding excuses. This had been her home for the first seventeen years of her life. Until Raif Dangerfield had shattered her illusions and driven her away. But that was eight years ago.

Dorian put him out of her mind as she drove along the familiar, tree-lined streets. Everything looked the same until she pulled up in front of her old family home. The house and yard had a neglected look, even though she paid a caretaker to come regularly to look after the property. It was time to sell it and cut her last ties to the past.

As she got out of the car and started up the front walk, someone called to her. A young woman ran across the street waving enthusiastically.

"Dorian! I wondered when you were coming back," she said breathlessly.

The two women embraced fondly. Sally Carter was Dorian's oldest friend. They'd gone through school together from kindergarten on.

"Why didn't you let me know you were coming?" Sally asked. "I would have aired out the house and stocked it with food."

"I didn't decide until the last minute," Dorian explained. "Things have been really hectic at work."

"That's the price of success." Sally gazed admiringly at her friend's beige linen suit and high-heeled Italian shoes. "You've certainly changed since the old days."

"That's what you said the last time you saw me." Dorian smiled. "It's only been a few months."

"I still can't get used to you. I love your hair this way, but I remembered you in jeans, with your hair in a ponytail."

Raif had always loved her long hair. He used to say it was the color of warm butterscotch, neither blond nor brown but a glowing shade somewhere in between. After they'd made love he would comb his fingers languidly through the long strands as she rested her cheek on his bare chest.

The first thing she'd done after leaving him was cut her hair in a symbolic gesture of independence. It seemed childish now that she'd become a successful executive in charge of her own life.

"You have a good memory." Dorian picked up her suitcase, and the two women walked up the path to the front door.

The house had a deserted air that affected both of them.

"We had some good times here," Sally said wistfully. "I suppose you're going to sell the place."

"It's the only sensible thing to do. I won't ever be coming back here to live."

"I guess not," Sally said dejectedly. "Why would you? I just wish you could spend a little time here, though. I miss you."

"I've asked you to visit me in Los Angeles. It's only a couple of hours away."

"I know, but Kenny doesn't like to be left alone."

"That's ridiculous," Dorian said crisply as she went around opening windows. "A woman shouldn't lose her identity when she gets married. You have a right to do what *you* want."

Sally slanted a look at her that contained a mixture of understanding and compassion. "You're right. Would you like to come over to my house for coffee?" she asked, changing the subject.

"I'm sure there's some here," Dorian said, leading the way to the kitchen.

Sally sat at the round oak table while Dorian filled an old-fashioned percolator with water and measured coffee from a canister.

"How long will you be staying?" Sally asked.

"I plan on two weeks, unless some crisis arises and I have to go back sooner."

"You're the boss. Can't you take off as long as you like?"

"Unfortunately it doesn't work that way."

Sally gazed at her speculatively. "You must meet a lot of high-powered men in your business."

"All unemployed. They come to me to find them jobs."

"What's that name they call people like you? Head hunters?"

Dorian laughed. "We prefer to be known as executive placement counselors."

"Your clients must be very dynamic men," Sally persisted. "We're not talking your ordinary shoe clerks, here."

"No. I deal with corporations that are looking for presidents and vice presidents, or at the least, national sales managers." Dorian rose to pour the coffee. "Speaking of jobs, is Ken still working for the Bailey Construction Company?"

"Off and on. Business is rather slow right now, but it will pick up."

Dorian was reaching for the sugar bowl so she didn't notice the shadow that crossed Sally's face. "That's what I love about Summerville. Nothing ever changes."

"I wouldn't say that. Kenny and I are expecting a big change in our lives. I'm pregnant."

"That's fantastic!" Dorian exclaimed. "I'm so happy for you."

"It's about time, don't you think? All our friends are on their second or third." Sally was chagrined at the suddenly withdrawn look on Dorian's face. "Not that having a baby is such a big deal," she added hastily. "Women do it all the time. Oh, God!" she groaned as soon as the words were out. "How could I have said that? I'm so sorry, Dorrie."

"It's all right," Dorian answered calmly. "That's ancient history. I haven't thought about it in years."

That was a lie. Although she didn't dwell on the past, Dorian often wondered about the baby she'd miscarried. It had been a boy. Would he have looked like his father, with Raif's black hair and laughing green eyes? She would never know.

"There's something I'd better tell you," Sally said uneasily. "Raif is back in town."

Dorian froze. She'd never expected to see him again. Never *wanted* to see him. His rejection had almost destroyed her. Even now, with all her achievements, the thought of meeting him face-to-face threw her into a panic.

Her lips felt stiff as she asked, "What's he doing here?"

"I don't know. He's living in his parents' old house. I haven't been by since he came back, but it was kind of a dump, if you remember. Raif's mother and dad left town a year or so ago, but they must not have sold the place."

"It sounds as if Raif is down on his luck," Dorian remarked casually.

"He can't be looking for a job here. There isn't much work for an engineer in Summerville."

Dorian hesitated a moment before asking, "How does he look?"

"Kind of tired. I don't know what he's been doing all these years. He left town right after you did."

"I wonder why he came back after all this time."

"Maybe he didn't have anywhere else to go."

Dorian would have sworn she was through caring what happened to Raif. Yet she couldn't help feeling a twinge. He had always been so capable, so in charge. It was difficult to imagine Raif beaten down by life.

"Anyway, I thought I'd better warn you so you'd be prepared," Sally continued. "In a town this small you're bound to run into each other."

"Not necessarily." Dorian's nerves were already jangling at the possibility. "I won't be here that long."

"In two weeks you can meet every living soul in Summerville." Sally laughed.

"Does he see the old crowd?" Dorian asked hesitantly.

"No, he keeps pretty much to himself. Dwight and Francine asked him to dinner a couple of times, but he put them off."

"Dwight was Raif's best friend."

Sally shrugged. "Raif could be sensitive about not having made good in the hard cruel world out there."

"What does he do with himself if he doesn't see anyone?" Dorian wanted to let the matter drop, but she couldn't.

Sally's voice was overly casual as she replied, "He isn't a complete recluse. Somebody saw him with Linda Kramer."

"I hope it wasn't her husband," Dorian commented waspishly.

"Linda and Sam were divorced about a year ago."

"How convenient. She was crazy about Raif in high school. Now she has a second crack at him."

Linda had tried every tactic in the book to get Raif away from Dorian, and she had a potent array of weapons. Even at seventeen her figure had been lushly provocative, an endowment she'd capitalized on by wearing tight sweaters. Linda had had her pick of boyfriends, but she'd gone after Raif with open determination, although in those days he hadn't been interested. Evidently he was now.

"Raif has changed a lot. Sometimes things work out better on the second try," Sally was saying quietly.

"They have my blessing. In fact, they deserve each other."

"I was talking about you and Raif. You're both more mature now. Maybe it could work this time. You were so much in love."

Dorian uttered a harsh laugh. "Is that why he left me when he had the chance?"

"You were the one who left *him*."

"What would you have done if the man you loved said your relationship had been a mistake? He wanted his freedom, so I gave it to him."

"I can't believe Raif actually wanted out. He was so concerned when you lost the baby."

Dorian stood up and carried the coffee cups to the sink. "That was a very painful episode in my life. I'd rather not discuss it, if you don't mind."

"Of course. I shouldn't have brought it up." Sally bit her lip as she looked at her friend's stiff back. "You'll have your hands full unpacking and getting settled," she remarked in a determinedly cheerful voice. "Come over to our house for dinner tonight."

"No, thanks. I might as well go marketing and get it over with."

"Please don't be angry with me, Dorrie." Sally's face reflected her unhappiness. "I only want what's best for you."

"I know." Dorian's tense figure relaxed and she managed a smile. "Give me a rain check on dinner, though. I really have a million things to do around here."

After Sally left, Dorian unpacked and changed to cream-colored slacks and a matching silk blouse, then scribbled a hasty marketing list. The excuse she'd given Sally had been valid. There was no food in the house except staples.

In spite of the many things she had to do at home, Dorian drove around the neighborhood, revisiting all the old landmarks. Central High with its ivy-covered clock tower, the malt shop across the street where the crowd used to gather at lunch period. Everyone had been so impressed when Raif came to join her for lunch. He was a senior in college then.

Raif had seemed destined for success in those days. He excelled at everything and his ambition was boundless. He used to talk about the things he would buy for Dorian someday, although all she wanted was him. Another dream he had was to move his parents out of their shabby house in the run-down neighborhood where he grew up. Raif was never ashamed of his background. He simply wanted his parents to have a better life.

Although she could never forgive Raif for failing her, Dorian could understand, on looking back, why he didn't want to be tied down. A whole world of opportunity awaited a young man who was free to go out and take advantage of it. Poor Raif. He had his chance, but he didn't measure up.

Dorian drove past the supermarket without slowing down. What she was about to do was foolish, but she might as well get this whole trip down memory lane over with.

Raif's neighborhood hadn't improved. Most of the houses needed paint, and the yards were largely neglected. Some had flower gardens, though, showing gallant pride in the face of adversity.

Dorian slowed as she turned into Raif's street, but she almost missed his house because it looked so different. A coat of white paint had been applied recently; the trim was black and the front door was lacquered Chinese red. Dorian stopped to read the house number, thinking perhaps she was on the wrong block.

When he heard the car stop, Raif jumped down from the large peach tree he'd been pruning. His mildly inquisitive glance turned to one of disbelief as he recognized Dorian.

She was merely startled at first, then her breathing almost stopped. Raif was naked to the waist, and his ragged jeans rode low on narrow hips, giving her a comprehensive look at his lean physique. The body she'd thought was so perfect before, was even more splendid now. It had hardened into a fluid composition of sinew and muscle, with no fat to mar its perfection.

Raif was the first to recover. Walking over to the car he said, "It *is* Dorian, isn't it?" His gaze moved from her face to her short feathery hairdo.

"I heard you were back," she said breathlessly.

His deeply tanned face creased in a smile. "How nice of you to look me up."

"I didn't expect... I mean, I was just driving by."

"You happened to be in the neighborhood?" His smile was mocking now.

"No, I—" Dorian clenched her jaw. It was absurd to let Raif affect her this way. She wasn't a lovesick high school girl anymore. "I was surprised to hear you'd returned to Summerville," she said evenly.

"I had a sudden urge to come home." His voice softened as he said, "I was sorry to hear about your parents' accident."

"It was a terrible blow. I was here for the funeral of course, but I couldn't force myself to come back again until now. I'm here to sell the house and dispose of their possessions."

"That's a tough job," he said sympathetically.

"Yes." She nodded. "Well, it was nice to see you." There didn't seem to be anything left to say.

"Don't rush off. Come inside for a drink."

"I don't think so, Raif."

"I'd really like you to see what I've done to the old place."

"The outside looks very nice."

"That's only the beginning. You have to see the rest," he urged.

Dorian couldn't believe she was doing this, but she got out of the car and followed him up the walk. Bricks had replaced the cracked concrete, and the small patches of lawn on either side of the path were neatly mowed.

Revisiting Raif's house was almost as poignant as returning to her own had been. Dorian remembered the many afternoons she'd visited with his mother in the kitchen while Raif was changing out of his football or baseball clothes after school. Mrs. Dangerfield was usually baking something that smelled wonderful.

Dorian braced herself for a rush of memories, but the living room didn't bring back any. The worn furniture had been replaced with tasteful, well-made pieces, and the formerly shabby room had been carpeted and draped.

"You really did make some changes," she exclaimed.

"My parents did the redecorating," he said. "I've been making some structural changes. Come and see how I enlarged the kitchen."

Dorian followed him into a room that used to be dark and cramped. Now it could have been a selling point in a model home. An outside wall had been moved back several feet, and skylights, cut in the ceiling, flooded the enlarged room with light. Every modern appliance made it a dream kitchen.

"*You* did this?" Dorian asked incredulously.

Raif looked gratified. "It came out pretty well, didn't it?"

"*Fabulous* is the word! But how did you know how to do all this? You're an engineer, not an architect."

"Designing houses isn't so different from building bridges. Anyway, you know me." He laughed. "I never recognized my own limitations."

Yes, Raif had always had boundless curiosity and confidence. He wanted to find out how everything worked, and then learn to do it himself. Maybe that was the trouble. He jumped around too much to be successful.

"You've done wonders with the house," she said quietly. "I'm surprised your mother wanted to leave after you fixed it all up for her."

"They have a bigger one now. It's on a golf course." Raif grinned. "Can you imagine my pop playing golf?"

Dorian decided his parents must have inherited money. "I hope your mother is still baking those delicious cookies. I'll never forget how good they tasted, right out of the oven."

"She was very fond of you," Raif said quietly. "She felt badly that you wouldn't see her after we broke up."

"It seemed best at the time."

"Running away from something is never a solution."

Dorian's chin shot up. "It was for us."

"Have you been happy all these years, Dorian?"

"Very happy," she said firmly. "Haven't you?"

"I concentrated on my work," he answered briefly. "I wasn't looking for happiness."

"What you really mean is commitment," she said bitterly.

"You still believe that?"

"It doesn't matter anymore." Digging her nails into her palms, she remarked brightly, "Actually when you look back, the whole thing was kind of funny. Can you ever forget the panic in town when it came out that the Reverend Felcher wasn't an ordained minister, and none of the marriages he performed were legal?"

"The other couples remarried," Raif said evenly.

Dorian had thought the pain was gone, but it wasn't. Suddenly the years melted away and she was seventeen again, confident of the future and her love for Raif. They had married right after graduation, she from high school and he from college. Her parents worried that she was too young, but Dorian knew her love for Raif was the real thing.

Besides, they'd made very mature decisions. She would get her college degree as planned, then work for a few years before taking time out to have a family. It didn't turn out that way.

At the end of summer, right before she was ready to register for college, Dorian discovered she was pregnant. Under the circumstances it would have been foolish to start the fall semester. The baby would arrive before she finished her first year.

Raif clearly had mixed feelings about the baby from the beginning. He pretended to be happy, but Dorian could sense he had reservations. She was so ecstatic, however, that his lack of enthusiasm didn't really register. Whenever he expressed fear that they would be missing out on all the carefree experiences their friends would enjoy, she laughed at the thought.

The roof caved in on Dorian's idyllic life when she miscarried, then discovered right afterward that she and Raif weren't even married. In her pain and grief she questioned everything she'd believed in, even Raif's devotion. Looking for reassurance, she asked him if he would have married her if he'd realized what marriage entailed. When he hesitated, her misery deepened, and when he said it might have been better if they'd waited, the bottom dropped out of her world.

Raif was watching the welter of emotions cross her expressive face. "It's pointless to relive the past," he said gently. "Nothing can change it, but at least we can be friends."

How could you have that pallid a relationship with someone you'd known intimately? Dorian was familiar with every hard angle of Raif's body. After all these years she could still recall the thrust of his loins, their shared passion, the final, thunderous burst of sensation that had left them spent in each other's arms.

She drew a deep breath to dispel the disturbing image. "To be perfectly honest, I don't feel very friendly toward you, Raif."

"I hoped after all this time you might have mellowed."

"Rejection is hard to swallow."

"I never rejected you, Dorian. It's inconceivable that you could have believed such a thing. I was only thinking of you."

"I'm sure you've convinced yourself of that."

"We were too young to get married," he said wearily, like a man repeating something he'd said often. "I knew it at the time, but I thought I could compensate for all you'd be missing—the proms, the dates with the current football hero."

"I never looked at another man after I met you," she said indignantly.

"Exactly. You had no chance to make comparisons, and—selfishly—I wanted to keep it that way. When you became pregnant, I was torn between joy and guilt. You were the one making all the sacrifices."

"I was thrilled about the baby!"

"You were seventeen years old," he answered roughly. "You had this rosy view of motherhood. The down side never occurred to you, the restrictions on your freedom, the responsibility."

"*You* were the one who didn't want to be saddled with those things," she flared.

Raif sighed. "I have a feeling of déjà vu."

"You're right. It's silly to go over the same ground again." She turned toward the door. "I love what you've done with the house. Good luck in it."

"Don't go. You haven't seen the new patio yet."

"Maybe another time. I have to stop at the market, and then I really must get home."

"You can spare a few minutes for a drink," he coaxed.

She shook her head. "It's too early in the day."

"I was thinking of a Dorian special." He smiled. "Do you still like root beer over coffee ice cream?"

"You remembered," she marveled. "It's been years since I even thought about those."

"I haven't forgotten anything about you," he said softly.

Dorian was suddenly painfully aware of Raif's blatant masculinity. He looked especially sexy in the tight jeans that outlined his powerful thigh muscles.

She forced a laugh. "You used to say root beer and coffee were a terrible combination. Don't tell me you've become a convert?"

"Only if I were stranded in the middle of the Sahara Desert." Raif had the refrigerator door open and was reaching inside. "I don't have any root beer and I'm out of ice cream. Will a cola do instead?" Before she could refuse, he took out two cans and handed one to her. "Let's take these outside where it's cooler. I haven't gotten around to installing air-conditioning yet."

Dorian was distracted by curiosity. "That sounds as though you intend to live here permanently," she commented, following him outside.

"I don't really have any plans at the moment." He pulled out a chair for her and raised a fringed canvas umbrella anchored in the middle of a wrought iron table. "Pretty nifty, huh?"

She refused to be led away from the subject. "What will you do in Summerville?"

He shrugged. "I'll wait and see what turns up."

"There isn't much work here for an engineer," Dorian said, echoing Sally's sentiment.

Raif smiled. "I'm adaptable. I've learned to be a jack-of-all-trades."

"Where have you been living all these years?"

"Different places." Before she could pin him down he asked, "How about you? What have you been doing since you left town?"

She glanced away. "Well...in the beginning I went to Los Angeles to stay with my aunt."

"I know. I tried to call you there."

Dorian had been too hurt and angry to talk to Raif at first, and Aunt Harriet was happy to act as a buffer. She had a low opinion of all men, having been jilted herself many years earlier.

"You wouldn't take any of my phone calls," Raif was saying.

"We had nothing to talk about."

"I'd say we had a lot. How could you simply cut me out of your life, Dorian?"

"It didn't bother you for long," she answered somberly. "After those first few weeks, you gave up."

"There wasn't much point in continuing to call. Your aunt was openly hostile, so when I couldn't reach you on the phone I wrote to you. But you never answered my letters."

Dorian gave him a startled look. "I never received any letters. Not even a card on my eighteenth birthday." That had really hurt.

"I sent you one, along with flowers."

"I didn't get those, either."

"Evidently your aunt didn't trust you not to weaken," he said ironically.

Would Aunt Harriet do such an underhanded thing? She would if she thought it was in her niece's best interests. Dorian felt a stab of regret. Their lives might be completely different if she'd known Raif was trying to make amends. Still, everything probably worked out for the best. She'd made something of her life out of the ruins.

"I also sent flowers when you graduated from U.C.L.A.," he said.

"Pink roses?"

He nodded. "At least you got those."

"But there was no card with them. I would have called or written to thank you."

"By then I didn't think you were interested in hearing from me. It was just something I wanted to do."

"They were lovely," she said softly. "It was very thoughtful of you."

"I'm not completely insensitive." He smiled.

Raif had been completely the opposite. He was always bringing her endearing little gifts, even when he could barely afford them. As she felt herself weakening, Dorian hardened her heart. That was a charming trait, but no substitute for dependability. Nothing could excuse the fact that he'd weaseled out when the opportunity had presented itself.

"How did you know when I graduated?" she asked.

"I kept track of you," he answered briefly. "Until I left the country, anyway."

That hadn't occurred to her. "Where did you go?"

"A lot of places." He brushed off the details as unimportant. "Why did you settle in Los Angeles instead of coming back to Summerville to live? Because you'd made friends there?" He was watching her intently.

Dorian knew what Raif was asking. Did someone special influence her decision? She would have walked naked down Main Street sooner than admit she'd never met a man who could take his place.

"I stayed on after graduation because I was offered an excellent job with a management consulting firm," she answered coolly. "After a couple of years I'd learned enough to start my own business."

He gazed at her admiringly. "You *look* like a successful businesswoman."

"I hung in there," she replied in a subtle rebuke.

"It also helps to know what you want," he said mildly.

"What happened to *your* dreams, Raif?" she asked slowly. "You had such grandiose plans."

"Sometimes you have to give up your dreams."

Dorian had fantasized about having the opportunity to flaunt her success in front of Raif. The fact that he was a failure should have made the triumph even sweeter, but it didn't. Their changed circumstances brought no pleasure.

"I'm sorry," she said awkwardly.

"Don't be. At least you got what *you* wanted."

"I suppose so," she said in a muted voice.

"I'm really proud of you."

"It's nice of you to say so, under the circumstances."

"Why wouldn't I be happy for you?" His voice deepened. "We go back a long way."

They were getting into dangerous territory. Dorian rose from her chair. "It's been nice seeing you again, Raif, but I really must get to work."

He walked through the house with her. "How long will you be in Summerville?"

"Probably two weeks."

"Then maybe we'll see each other again."

"I doubt it. I have a big job ahead of me, disposing of all the stuff in the house. My parents lived there almost thirty years."

"I remember it well." He opened the car door for her, then bent down to lean crossed arms on the open window. "We used to make out on the porch swing, and your father would come to the door if the chain stopped squeaking." Raif grinned. "I learned how to wiggle it with one hand while I kissed you."

Dorian smiled unwillingly. "At least that kept you too busy to seduce me."

"My intentions were honorable from the first moment I saw you," he said huskily. "You had on a pink sweater and your hair was in a ponytail." His long fingers combed through the feathery curls at the nape of her neck.

A little shiver traveled down her spine. "That was a long time ago." She started the motor. "I have to go, Raif." She drove away before he could try to delay her.

He stood at the curb, thumbs hooked in the waistband of his jeans, resting his weight on one hip as he stared at the receding car. She took a last look at him in the rear-view mirror before turning the corner and putting him out of her life.

Dorian drove home like a robot, all her thoughts centered on Raif. It had been a mistake to go by his house, and an even bigger one to go inside. There could never be anything between them again, but he still had the power to disturb her mightily. The memories he stirred up added to her distress.

Dorian was so preoccupied that she forgot to stop at the market. When she arrived home and realized the omission, she didn't feel like going back. There were some canned goods in the pantry. That would have to do for dinner.

After changing into denims she decided to tackle the garage first. It would take days to clear out all the dried-up paint cans, warped lawn chairs and other useless items that had accumulated through the years. The garage was also the least likely place to hold unwanted memories.

Her reasoning was sound, but the painful flashbacks recurred on their own. Further proof that she should have stayed away from Raif. Why did he have to look so virile? He was always able to rouse her senses. Their sex life had been perfect even if nothing else about their marriage turned out to be.

She would never forget the first time they made love. He'd been so gentle, so patient, teaching her how incredibly beautiful the physical side of love could be with someone you cared about.

Dorian grabbed a carton and started throwing old magazines into it, willing herself to concentrate on the job. But it didn't work. Conjectures kept swirling around in her mind like a swarm of stinging hornets. Had she made the right decision eight years ago? Could they have made a go of their marriage? Was success worth the price she paid for it?

When the unanswerable questions became intolerable, Dorian returned to the house. With a look of grim determination, she dialed her office number in Los Angeles.

Her secretary, Karen Pasquale, answered in a slightly harried tone of voice. "Good afternoon, Merrill Agency. Can you hold please?"

When she came back on the line, Dorian asked, "What's going on? Why are you answering the phones?"

"Maria is out sick," Karen answered, referring to the switchboard operator. "And so is that new girl you hired to do the paperwork. I don't think she's going to work out."

"Can't you get help from the other secretaries?" Dorian employed three placement counselors who all had their own assistants.

"They're busy, too. It seems half the executives in the country have either gotten the ax or suspect they're about to, so they're all job hunting."

"We don't say they've been fired, we refer to it as a termination of corporate networking," Dorian said dryly.

"I know, I know. Whatever. Anyway, it's good for business, but terrible on the help."

Dorian chewed her lip. "Maybe I'd better come back."

"No, we can handle things here. Stay and take care of your business in Summerville. It's something that has to be done, and you're the only one who can do it."

"I *would* like to sell the place and get if off my mind," Dorian admitted.

"It must be rough having to get rid of all the things that once meant so much to you," Karen said sympathetically.

"Harder than I thought it would be," Dorian answered soberly.

"I know, but you can't live in the past. Get through it as fast as possible, and keep reminding yourself of the terrific life you have in L.A."

"I'll do that. Thanks for the pep talk." Dorian changed the subject abruptly. "Have you heard from Warren Forsythe? How did his interview go with InterGlobal Technology?"

"Extremely well. They called me to double-check some points on his resumé, but I got the impression it was only a formality. I'm sure he has the job."

"Good. How about Capital Industries? Did they make up their mind about a counseling service for the executives taking early retirement?"

Karen laughed. "That's another polite term we use for being forced out."

The two women talked business for another ten minutes. Finally Dorian said, "I won't keep you on the phone any longer. I know you're busy. Is there anything you want to ask me about before we hang up?"

"Only one thing. Hadn't I better do something about the cocktail party?"

"What cocktail party?" Dorian asked blankly.

"The one you're hosting for the Executive Management Association. Their convention starts in ten days."

"Oh, good Lord!" Dorian exclaimed. "I meant to make the arrangements before I left and I completely forgot."

"No problem, I can do it. Where do you want to hold the party? In a hotel?"

"I'd prefer a restaurant. It's a more personal atmosphere. See if you can get the private room at Spandelli's. I hope it isn't too late," Dorian fretted.

"I'll use a little gentle persuasion. Corso Spandelli owes us a favor," Karen said reassuringly. "Anything special you want on the menu?"

"Order the duck sausage pizza, and those creole chicken wings with the hot sauce. But I want the buffet table to include some standard food as well. Smoked salmon is always a favorite, and roast beef on little slices of French bread. Tell Corso to station someone at the table to carve the beef. I don't want it presliced."

After they'd discussed the details at length, Dorian hung up feeling energized. Her invitations would be almost universally accepted. Executives and their wives from all over the country would be eager to visit the famous restaurant that was mentioned frequently in the media from coast to coast. The party was bound to generate a lot of new business.

Not that she needed it. The Merrill Agency was solidly successful. Not a lot of women were in her tax bracket—or men either. Certainly not Raif.

Dorian was annoyed with herself for letting him intrude on her thoughts again. He was a romantic leftover from her girlhood. She was a woman now, with everything she needed to make her happy.

Chapter Two

Dorian settled down to work in earnest the next morning. She was up early, despite a restless night. Or maybe because of it. She was eager to banish the erotic episodes with Raif that had dominated her dreams.

Cleaning out the garage was pure drudgery. Dorian filled endless cartons with debris that was useless to anyone. Clothing and assorted bric-a-brac would go to charity, but the out and out junk was a problem. How would she get it to the city dump? Her sports car was scarcely the answer.

A solution presented itself when Raif arrived unexpectedly. In the middle of the morning he drove a battered old truck into her driveway. Dorian felt her pulse beat faster as he swung himself out of the high seat in one lithe movement and ambled toward her. Damn the man! Even his walk was sexy.

"I thought you might need some help," he said.

"You must be clairvoyant," she answered. "I have tons of stuff to get rid of, and your truck would be a blessing."

"That's what I figured. I brought some cartons along in case you didn't have enough."

"I don't. I'm running out already." Dorian glanced around the still-littered garage. "I can't believe how much stuff my parents accumulated."

"That's what happens when you live in one place for a long time." Something in Raif's voice made her look at him more closely, but he was gazing at her father's work-bench. "You aren't going to throw away those tools, are you?"

"I was. You can have them if you like."

"Great! They've hardly been used."

Raif's delight in the old tools really hurt Dorian. He must be worse off than she thought. "Feel free to take anything you like," she said casually. "I'm just going to toss it all out."

He switched his attention to a battered old desk. "That desk could be refinished and put to good use. The Senior Citizen's Center would be happy to get it."

Dorian felt a touch of impatience. "Is that all you have to do with your time?"

"What's wrong with helping people out?" he asked mildly.

You need help yourself! she wanted to shout. Restraining herself, she asked, "Don't you get bored just puttering around?"

"I consider it enjoying a well-earned vacation. Something you could use." He looked at her appraisingly. "You need to take time out to smell the flowers...while there still are some."

"That's a luxury you can't afford if you want to get ahead in business," she stated firmly. "Someone is always right there waiting to knock you off the ladder."

He examined her face as though seeing her for the first time. "Success means a lot to you, doesn't it?"

"It's the most important thing," she replied simply.

"That's sad."

Her chin shot up. "Save your pity for someone who needs it. I know exactly what I want out of life, and how to get it."

"Meaning money, I presume."

"Not for its own sake, but money *is* a measure of success."

"What do you do when you aren't devoting yourself to being a success?"

The question caught her off guard. "I . . . well, I . . . lots of things. My life is very full."

"I hope so," Raif said gently.

"I can tell you're not convinced, but you're wrong. Yes, I work long hours, but that's what I enjoy."

"How about human relationships? Not necessarily with the opposite sex. I mean getting involved with people, helping them."

"That's what I do all day long. It's my business."

"We're not even speaking the same language," Raif muttered. He bent over and picked up a cardboard box. "I'll load these full cartons onto the truck."

Dorian had an uncomfortable suspicion that Raif was jealous of her success. In a desire to prove her worth, had she overdone it? She wanted to make some kind of amends, but their situation was tricky. What could she say? I'm sorry I made it and you didn't?

By the time Raif had finished lugging the heavy cartons out to the truck, he seemed to have worked off his resentment. Or at least gotten it under control. He was completely relaxed again, able to tease her about being an executive.

"I haven't heard a coffee break mentioned," he complained. "How do you keep your help?"

"That's the trouble with you young fellows today. All you're interested in are the incentives."

"You provide plenty of those." His admiring glance swept over her slim figure, from the tight jeans that outlined her bottom, to the T-shirt that hugged her breasts.

Dorian felt a pleasurable warmth which she concealed under a light tone. "Flattery won't get you a coffee break."

They worked together amiably from then on, with no undercurrents. After a couple of hours she put a hand on the small of her back and groaned. "I may never be able to straighten up again."

"That's the trouble with you delicate flowers nowadays." Raif grinned, getting back at her. "You wilt when you have to do an honest day's work."

"Even a flower gets a drink of water once in a while."

She bent at the waist and braced herself with both hands on the work bench, lowering her head. Raif came up behind her as silently as a cat. When he slid an arm around her waist, Dorian stiffened automatically, but his intention was merely to rub her back.

"This will make you feel better," he promised.

His strong fingers dug into her tight muscles, bringing a mixture of pleasure and pain. The soreness gradually changed to a warm glow under his rhythmic strokes, and her groans became a satisfied purr.

"Don't stop. That feels so good." She sighed.

Raif's hand stilled for an instant, then glided lower. His fingers slipped inside the waistband of her jeans and smoothed the tiny golden hairs along her spine. They reacted instantly to his touch.

"You used to say that to me under different circumstances," he murmured.

Dorian straightened up and reached back to pull his hand away, but his arm was still around her waist. Their bodies now conformed closely, his front to her back. She held herself stiffly in his embrace, appalled at the sudden rush of desire that flooded through her.

"Let go of me, Raif," she said tautly.

He complied at once. "Did that help?" he asked in a voice that held only interested inquiry.

Raif was evidently not affected by her, in spite of his sensual reference to their former lovemaking. He'd meant it as a joke, no doubt, Dorian thought indignantly. Raif always did have an overdeveloped sense of humor!

She moved away, arching her back. "Yep, good as new." Her voice was as casual as his, but she avoided looking at him.

"I'd advise you to take a break, anyway."

"You're probably right. Let's knock off for lunch."

"I thought you'd never ask." He grinned.

"I treat my help well, in spite of your scurrilous remarks. First I have to go to the market, though."

"All I want is a sandwich," he assured her. "Don't go to any trouble."

"Did you ever have a sandwich made on stale crackers? I don't have any bread."

"In that case, let's go to Tony's for a hamburger."

"I really have to market or those stale crackers will be my dinner. I won't be gone long."

"I'll go with you," he offered.

"Okay. I'll change and be right back."

"You look fine just the way you are. We're only going to the market."

She looked down at her outfit doubtfully. "I'm kind of grubby and I didn't put on any makeup this morning."

"You don't need it. This is Summerville, not Beverly Hills. People don't get dressed up to go to the grocery store."

Dorian smiled ruefully. "I keep forgetting there are still places where you can be yourself. I'm used to putting up a front every time I step out the door."

"Maybe you should spend more time here," Raif said gravely.

She shook her head. "Haven't you heard? You can't go home again."

"*I* did."

Because you gave up, she answered silently. You let the world beat you, but that's not going to happen to me. Since she couldn't very well say those things, Dorian dusted off her jeans while she remarked, "This is no time for a philosophical discussion. I didn't have any breakfast, and I can't concentrate on an empty stomach."

Raif frowned. "You haven't changed. I could never get you to eat anything in the morning."

"I make up for it at lunch. Come on, let's buy out the store."

While Raif pushed the shopping cart, Dorian filled it with a variety of frozen and convenience foods, enough to last a week so she wouldn't have to make another trip for a while. Raif viewed her selections with growing disapproval.

"Is this the way you eat all the time?" he demanded.

"What's wrong with it?"

"Everything! All that stuff has preservatives in it."

"Well, certainly. That's so it won't spoil."

"If you ate real food, you wouldn't have to worry about shelf life."

"This *is* real food. Don't tell me you're into one of those weird diets consisting solely of alfalfa sprouts and kiwi fruit?"

"That would be better for you than the artificially flavored, colored and processed junk you have there," he said, gesturing disdainfully. "It's bad for your health, and the packaging clutters up the environment."

"What am I supposed to eat? I don't have time to cook from scratch."

"How long does it take to shove a chicken in the oven and bake a potato?"

"I should have left you home," she said crossly. "You're worse to take shopping than a little kid!"

His frown changed to a smile. "How can you say that? I haven't pestered you for chocolate crunch cereal or passion fruit popsicles."

"No, you've just tried to ruin my appetite for everything that tastes good."

"I'm merely trying to make you take better care of yourself."

They bickered amicably as they strolled up and down the aisles.

When Dorian had finished shopping and they were waiting in the checkout line, Raif said, "I'll take care of this. You can bring the car around."

"Why should you pay for my groceries?" she objected.

"I'm going to help you eat some of them."

"You're being ridiculous, Raif."

"Don't make a federal case out of nothing." He put his hand in his pocket, then withdrew it and tried the other side. When that one came out empty, too, he patted his back pockets muttering, "Don't tell me I forgot my wallet."

"It doesn't matter. I wasn't going to let you pay, anyway."

"What a stupid thing to do," he said, berating himself.

Dorian felt acutely sorry for him. Fortunately a diversion saved his pride. A woman who had just entered the store called out to him.

"Hi, Raif. So this is where you hang out. I tried to return your call, but you're never home."

Dorian glanced over automatically. The woman had long blond hair that cascaded to her shoulders in shining waves. She was wearing a blue silk dress, high-heeled white pumps, and her makeup was flawless. Dorian scowled as she recognized Linda Kramer.

Linda came over to the checkout stand. "Have you had lunch yet?" she asked Raif. "I'd love to share a pizza at Rudy's."

Dorian had ducked in back of the woman ahead of her. She wouldn't have welcomed a reunion with Linda under any circumstances, and certainly not now when the other woman looked so picture perfect, while *she* was such a mess.

Raif grasped her arm and pulled her into view. "Sorry. Dorian and I are going to grab a quick sandwich and get back to cleaning her garage."

"Dorian!" Linda squealed, as though greeting her best friend. "I didn't see you there. When did you get back?"

"Yesterday." Even to her own ears that sounded curt, so Dorian added, "I've barely had time to unpack."

"I was so shocked to hear about your parents' accident. You must have been devastated. That drunken driver who hit them deserves a stiff sentence."

The line had moved and it was now Dorian's turn at the cashier. As Raif started to unload the contents of the cart onto the counter, she muttered to him, "I can do that. Take her away somewhere before she tells everybody in the market my life story."

"Okay, I'll wait for you by the entrance."

Dorian was irrationally annoyed that he followed her instructions so promptly. She fumed silently as the two moved over to the door, out of earshot but still in sight. She could see Linda's intimate little smile and the proprietary way she put her hand on Raif's arm. The indulgent look on his face indicated the interest between them was far from one-sided.

It took the grocery clerk a long time to ring up all the items in Dorian's cart, but Linda showed no signs of going on about her business. She and Raif were deep in conversation. When all the food was bagged, Dorian reluctantly wheeled the cart in their direction. She would have gone out to the car without stopping for meaningless chitchat, but they were blocking the door.

Raif had a smile for her, too. He must be feeling like a pasha with a harem, Dorian thought sourly. But if he expected her to compete for him again, he was sadly mistaken.

"All finished?" he asked unnecessarily.

Linda turned to her. "I'm so glad I bumped into you today. This is just like old times."

"Scarcely." Dorian no longer cared if she sounded curt.

Linda laughed slightly. "I guess there have been a few changes since dear old Central High. *You* certainly look different. I never would have recognized you."

Dorian resisted the urge to try and make her hair more presentable. "I can't say the same about you. You're exactly as I remembered you."

Linda slanted a merry glance at Raif. "I'm not sure that's a compliment."

"Why wouldn't it be?" he asked blandly.

"Dorian knows I was crazy about you in the old days."

"We were all very immature then," Dorian said in a pinched voice.

"Our choices did turn out to be... Sam and I, you and Raif. But I never look back. Not when the future is so bright," Linda said complacently.

"You're very fortunate." Dorian's jaw set grimly. "This has been fun, but you'll have to excuse me. My frozen food is thawing."

"Before you rush off I want to talk to you about something," Linda said. "Raif told me you're selling your parent's house. I'd love to have the listing."

"Linda is a real estate agent," Raif explained.

Dorian gave him a look of acute dislike. "I don't suppose you alerted any of the other agents in town."

"I hope not," Linda answered before he could. "I'd like to have an exclusive. It's really to your advantage. You get more personal attention that way."

"But less prospective buyers," Dorian replied. "I plan to offer the property to all the realtors on a multiple-listing basis."

"They won't have the same incentive to push your house," Linda objected.

Dorian shrugged. "That's my decision."

"You're making a mistake. An agent with an exclusive will work much harder for you. Explain business practices to her," Linda appealed to Raif.

Dorian's temper almost flared out of control. "No one has to give me advice when it comes to business," she stated icily. "I am the head of a successful and respected placement agency that I built entirely on my own."

"I wouldn't consider offering you advice," Raif said quietly.

Linda looked from one to the other. "I didn't mean to sound patronizing," she said uncertainly.

"I'm sure Dorian realized we both admire her." Raif grasped the handle of the grocery cart. "See you later, Linda. Got to go before the ice cream melts." He smiled at Dorian.

She didn't return his smile, nor did she say a word all the way to the parking lot. While Raif loaded the groceries into the trunk of the sports car, Dorian slid behind the wheel. When he climbed into the passenger seat next to her, she started the motor and drove away, staring straight ahead.

"These little cars weren't meant for long legs like mine," Raif commented, trying to get comfortable.

"You didn't have to come along," she answered without glancing around.

"It's lucky I did."

Dorian scowled at the passing cars. "That's right. You would have missed meeting up with your biggest admirer."

"I meant, because I was here to help you with all the grocery bags," he explained patiently.

"Your good deed was amply rewarded."

Raif sighed, giving up the pretense that nothing unpleasant had occurred. "I realize you've never liked Linda, but did you have to make it so obvious?"

Dorian looked at him then, her eyes shooting sparks of blue fire. "The woman insulted my intelligence! What did you expect me to do? That bargain-basement Marilyn Monroe barely made it through high school. The only subject she ever got an A in was sex education."

He smothered a smile. "People do change in eight years. You did."

"That's another thing," Dorian flared. "She couldn't resist commenting on how messy I look."

"I didn't hear that."

"You wouldn't," she replied witheringly. "I never should have listened to you when you said everyone goes around looking like this."

"Is that what's bothering you?" His voice deepened. "On her best day, Linda couldn't hope to compare to you."

Dorian would have been more gratified if she hadn't seen the intimate look they'd exchanged in the market. "Don't *you* insult my intelligence, too. Linda might not be bright, but she's a beautiful, sexy woman."

"You're a lot sexier." His gaze traveled lingeringly over Dorian's slim figure.

"You're wasting your charm on me," she said shortly. "Linda would be more receptive. But you probably know that already."

He studied her with hidden speculation that he covered with a light tone. "Surely you don't expect me to kiss and tell."

The thought of Raif making love to Linda was intolerable. "I don't give a damn *what* you do!" she burst out.

"That's where we differ. I care very much about your welfare," he answered quietly.

"Then you should be more perceptive."

"Granted. I've made a great many mistakes where you're concerned, but I was hoping we could resurrect our friendship, if nothing else. We were friends before we were lovers."

Dorian's anger was replaced by a melancholy sense of loss. She pulled into her driveway and cut the motor before replying. "I'd like to be friends again, but I don't know if it's possible."

"The decision is up to you." He held out his hand for the key to the trunk. "I'll take your groceries into the house, and then I'll leave you alone."

"Don't go!" she said impulsively, then covered up with a smile. "Who will help me finish cleaning the garage?"

His expression was unreadable. "I'll send over a handyman."

Dorian knew if she let Raif go now, he wouldn't be back. That was probably the wisest course for both of them, but she couldn't let it happen.

"I want you to stay, Raif." She stared at the license plate on his truck to avoid looking at him. "I'm sorry for being such a shrew. I know it's childish to resent Linda after all these years, and I certainly have no right to inquire into your love life."

"Does that mean I have your blessing?" he ask dryly.

Dorian couldn't help herself. "If that's the best you can do."

Raif began to laugh. "That's the Dorian I remember. For a moment there, I was afraid you were turning into a saint."

"You know me better than that," she said ruefully.

"I used to know everything about you," he answered softly.

Their eyes held, as memories surfaced for both of them, sweet, moving memories that left Dorian unspeakably sad. Why couldn't she remember the bad times? The sight and sound and smell of Raif banished those.

She dragged her eyes away from his. "I'd better fix lunch so we can get back to work."

Raif helped her unload the bags in the kitchen. While Dorian made sandwiches he put the frozen food in the freezer and stacked canned goods in the pantry. It was such a cozy domestic scene that Dorian felt a further pang. This was the way they used to share such little tasks.

"Do you still like mustard and mayonnaise on your ham sandwiches?" she asked, to dispel the fruitless thought. "Or are they on your hit list, too? I hope you'll overlook the fact that I didn't bake the bread or cure the ham personally."

"I'll make an exception this time, as long as it doesn't happen again."

"Seriously, Raif. When did you get on a health kick? You're not sick or anything, are you?" she asked anxiously.

"I'm strong as a bull," he assured her. "And I'm not into trendy diets. I do believe in eating wholesome food because it makes good sense. The only thing I'm rabid about is the environment."

"Preservatives are bad for the environment?" she asked uncertainly.

"Pesticides certainly are, and gasoline emissions. But a major culprit is the destruction of the rain forests. That definitely contributes to the global warming trend."

"The ordinary person can't do anything about that," Dorian protested.

"That's where you're wrong. Everyone can pitch in. We need to use the world's resources sensibly instead of squandering them. We're spending our children's future." When her lashes fluttered down, Raif groaned. "Dorian, I'm sorry. That was insensitive."

"It's all right," she murmured.

"I'm afraid I get carried away sometimes," he said remorsefully.

"You were always passionate. I mean, you always cared deeply about things," she corrected herself hastily.

"I still do."

A small moment of silence fell as the past became vivid for both of them. Dorian was grateful when the telephone rang and broke the spell. It was her secretary in Los Angeles.

"I called to put your mind at ease about the cocktail party," Karen said. "Everything is arranged."

"Did you get the private room at Spandelli's?"

"After a little arm twisting. Although, for what this party will cost, we're doing *him* a favor."

"The cost isn't important," Dorian said crisply. "It's a business expense. Did Corso have any other suggestions concerning the menu?"

"Only one. He wants to stick with giant prawns instead of a variety of seafood. Crab legs are frozen at this time of year and oysters are chancy, even though he has them flown in."

"Then by all means skip the oysters and crab. But how about some lobster with the shrimp?"

After discussing a few more details, Dorian hung up. Raif had finished making their sandwiches and was putting the plates on the table.

He looked up with interest. "That's quite a party you're planning. I'm impressed."

She shrugged. "It isn't difficult when you can delegate all the work."

"You've learned the secret of being an executive."

"I suppose so," she answered uncomfortably.

"That's something I could never master. I have to get involved in all the details of a project."

"Everyone isn't cut out to be an executive. You have other talents."

He smiled slowly. "I'm glad you remember."

Dorian's nerves tightened at the frank sensuality in his glance. She set a jar of pickles on the table with a thump.

"This has to stop, Raif! You've been throwing out these suggestive remarks since yesterday, and I won't put up with it any longer. How can we hope to be friends if you keep harassing me this way?"

"I didn't realize that's what I was doing. Memories are unavoidable under the circumstances, but I'll keep them to myself now that I know they bother you."

"That wasn't what I said," she replied carefully. "If you reminisced about parties we'd been to or friends we used to see, it would be different. But you keep alluding to the personal side of our relationship, and that's all behind us."

"You're right, as usual. From now on I'll pretend we were casual acquaintances. Will that be satisfactory?"

Dorian gritted her teeth at the irony in his voice. "It would be an improvement."

"Okay, you've got it. Can I still call you by your first name?" When she gave him a quelling look, Raif grinned. "Merely trying to establish the boundaries."

She smiled reluctantly. "Just don't step over them anymore and we'll get along fine."

Raif kept his word all through lunch. Although he continued to show interest, it was in an acceptable fashion. He questioned Dorian about her business, asking whether she was paid by the employer or the employee, and if being fired from a previous job was a mark against her clients.

Usually Dorian enjoyed talking about her work, but not with Raif. The vast economic gap between them was too apparent. His probing questions made her even more uncomfortable. Was Raif going to ask her to find him a job? That would be the crowning indignity for him.

Dorian desperately wanted to change the subject, but the ones that occurred to her were tricky. They all involved shared experiences. Getting Raif to talk about himself wasn't a solution either. Her desire was to avoid embarrassing him. Finally she found a neutral topic, the magnitude of packing up the possessions of a lifetime, and what to do with them.

"I hope to sell the house furnished," she remarked. "But that still leaves a lot to dispose of, like linens and pots and pans, that sort of thing."

"The Senior Citizen's Center will take part of the kitchen equipment off your hands."

"You seem very interested in them. How did you get involved?"

"My parents suggested I lend a hand. Some of the group are friends of theirs."

"That's just the point. They're a different generation. What do you have in common with them?"

"Age isn't really important. They're nice people, and I like them," he answered simply. "I drop around to help out with various projects."

Dorian didn't attempt to mask her impatience with Raif. A lot of people suffered reverses; that didn't mean they folded their hands and gave up. "Don't you have anything better to do with your time?"

"I can't think of anything," he replied calmly.

"You're a little young to retire."

"I'm one of the lucky ones." He grinned. "I can do what I feel like."

"Does that mean you have enough money to last the rest of your life...if you don't live too long?" she asked dryly.

He shrugged. "People put too much emphasis on money. The important thing is to enjoy life."

"You enjoy doing nothing?"

"Nobody does. That's a problem the elderly face...inertia. They need to get out and interact with people—all kinds of people, not merely those their own age. Most of them are eager to get involved, but society has largely turned its back on them. It's a shame the way we isolate our senior citizens, as though old age is a communicable disease."

"You can't remedy the situation all by yourself," Dorian pointed out.

"That's an excuse too many of us use. For everything."

"You may be right, but we have to take charge of our own lives. There must be all kinds of projects they could become involved in."

"I'd be grateful if you could name just one."

Dorian pondered for a moment. "What kind of facilities does the Center have?"

"It's a small building that used to be a nursery school, quite nice really. I painted the place for them, but it still needs some fixing up."

"One solution I can think of is to start a nursery school. Working mothers are desperate for a place to leave their children, and the Center is already set up for the purpose."

"I'm afraid older people don't have the energy or the physical capability to chase after a bunch of toddlers."

"I suppose that's true. Well, how about older children, the latch-key kids? Why not create a place where they can drop by after school? Their parents would be grateful, and the kids would love to come if there was a CD player and some books and video games. Everyone would benefit. It would be like having an extended family of grandchildren."

Raif gazed at her thoughtfully. "That sounds like a fantastic idea, but I wonder if some of the group might object to all the noise and commotion."

"It would only be for a few hours in the afternoon. Anyone who minded could leave by three o'clock. The rest could stay and find out how much the younger generation has to offer." She flashed him a smile. "Both sides might get a liberal education."

Raif's face wore a look of excitement now. "It would keep them young. Dorian, I could kiss you."

"Is that my commission?" She was amazed to hear the invitation in her voice.

But Raif was too charged up to recognize it. "Will you come down to the Center with me and talk to Carrie Madison? She more or less runs things around there. You could look the place over and give her some ideas about how to get started."

"I really can't spare the time, Raif."

His animation fled. "I keep forgetting you're a high-priced executive now. Your time is worth money."

"That's not fair! I gave you the idea. It's up to you to make it work."

"You're quite right, and I'm grateful to you." He stood and carried their plates to the sink. "We'd better get back to work."

Dorian's mouth thinned in exasperation. "You can see for yourself how much I have to do around here."

"That's why I suggested we get started," he replied evenly.

"Stop treating me like a recalcitrant child," she stormed. "I hate it! That's what you used to do every time I disagreed with you."

"Not every time. Only when you were wrong." A smile glimmered behind his remote expression.

"I suppose *you* were always right?" she challenged.

"Obviously not or we'd still be married," he answered quietly. "But if we begin on that subject we really won't get anything accomplished."

Dorian watched moodily as Raif stacked the plates in the dishwasher. His good opinion shouldn't mean anything to her, but strangely enough it did.

"Oh, all right. I'll go to your precious Center with you," she grumbled.

"That isn't necessary. I don't want you to feel pressured."

"I said I'd go, and I will. But this is the last time I'm going to offer," she warned. "Take it or leave it."

"Then I accept with pleasure." His face relaxed in a smile. "Don't look so grim. Who knows? You might even enjoy yourself."

The afternoon passed swiftly in spite of the grubby work. Raif's company made the job more enjoyable, and certainly a lot easier. He lifted heavy cartons, threadbare tires and an old lawn mower as if they were toys. Dorian's eyes strayed often to watch the rippling muscles play across his bare back. When the afternoon sun heated the garage, Raif had stripped off his T-shirt.

Sally stopped by late in the day. "When you finish here, how would you like to come over and clean out *my* garage?" she joked.

Raif shook his head. "This is strictly a labor of love. For old times' sake," he added blandly.

"Raif has been invaluable," Dorian commented hastily.

Sally appraised his glistening torso. "You're lucky. I'll bet his services are in great demand."

Dorian glanced quickly at her watch. "Golly, is it that late already? I was hoping to finish in here this afternoon."

"You've done enough for one day," Sally said. "Why don't you knock off and come over to my house for dinner? I'm calling in your rain check."

"That's a good idea," Raif advised Dorian. "No sense in driving yourself to the limit. I'll come back tomorrow and we'll polish off the rest of this stuff."

"You're invited to dinner, too, Raif," Sally told him.

He looked pleased. "Thanks. I was getting tired of my own cooking."

"Is that the only inducement?" Sally grinned at him mischievously.

"Plus good company, of course," he answered with the same glint of deviltry.

"You'd better go home and get cleaned up," Dorian said abruptly.

"Right. What time do you want me there?" Raif asked Sally.

"Come over as soon as you're ready. We'll have a drink on the patio while Kenny fires up the barbecue. Nothing fancy."

"Sounds great," he said. "See you shortly."

After Raif left, Dorian frowned at her friend. "You're as obvious as an elephant hiding behind a chain-link fence."

"I don't know what you're talking about," Sally replied innocently.

"Don't hand me that! Why did you invite Raif to dinner?"

"Because he's an old friend, and he was here. It wouldn't have been very polite to exclude him."

"That's not the reason and you know it. You're trying to play Cupid, but your intentions are misguided. I told you Raif and I were through."

"You looked remarkably compatible just now."

"Appearances are deceiving. He was simply helping me out."

"You mean you were only using him."

"Yes. No! That's a rotten thing to say." Dorian drew a deep breath. "Raif very kindly offered his assistance and I accepted. Everything is over between us, but that doesn't mean we can't be friends."

Sally's curiosity overrode her skepticism. "How did he even know you were in town? You just arrived yesterday. Did you phone him?"

"Certainly not. I . . . we happened to be in the market at the same time." That wasn't a lie.

"How fortunate," Sally murmured. "Well, as long as you're on such good terms, I can't see why you'd object to having dinner with Raif."

"I don't object. I simply want to make our relationship perfectly clear."

"Got it. Merely friends, nothing else."

"Exactly. So don't trot out the photo album tonight, and no reminiscing about the good old days."

"Maybe you'd better write out a list of dos and don'ts," Sally remarked dryly. "Or better yet, a list of safe subjects. Right now the only thing I'm sure of is the weather, but that won't get us past the salad course."

"Just don't try to get Raif and me back together again."

Sally dropped her bantering tone. "If that's the way you want it. But you two sure looked good together. Okay, I won't mention it again," she added hurriedly after a look at Dorian's expression. "See you later."

Dorian went into the house to shower, trying to dismiss Sally's sentimental words. This whole thing was getting out of hand and she had to put a stop to it. But how? She was committed to dinner with Raif tonight, he was coming over tomorrow, and she'd promised to go the Center with him at some future date. At this rate she might wind up seeing him every day of her stay in Summerville.

The prospect wasn't as grim as it should have been. After all, Dorian rationalized, it was only for two weeks. Smiling unconsciously, she reached for the bottle of shampoo and stepped into the shower.

Chapter Three

Raif hadn't arrived yet when Dorian walked across the street to the Carters'. After a fond reunion with Ken, whom she'd always liked, they all went outside to the patio.

"Los Angeles agrees with you," Ken remarked, gazing at Dorian admiringly. "You look terrific."

"Thanks. That's what I call being a good host," she answered lightly.

"No, really. You've come a long way from Summerville, baby. I'll bet you can't wait to get back to L.A."

"I wouldn't say that. Summerville is a nice little town."

He made a derogatory sound. "*Little* being the operative word."

"Big isn't necessarily better," Dorian argued. "If you had to fight the traffic every day and put up with the constant pressure and high prices, you'd appreciate what you have here."

"Prices are high everywhere, but at least there are opportunities in the city. The whole economy isn't dependent on a few industries."

Dorian looked at him curiously. "You and Sally are the last people I'd expect to leave Summerville. Are you considering pulling up roots?"

"Of course not," Sally answered for him in a sharp voice. "You'd better start the barbecue, Kenny."

"Raif isn't here yet," he objected.

"He will be soon, and you know how long it takes the coals to burn down properly."

"Do I tell you when to turn your stove on?" Ken grumbled good-naturedly as he went to follow his wife's instructions.

When he'd disappeared into the garden shed for a bag of charcoal, Dorian asked, "Is Ken getting restless here?"

"Not really. He's just concerned about the slowdown in the economy. Small towns don't bounce back as fast as urban areas."

"You mentioned that business is off at the construction company. Has it affected Ken?" Dorian looked at her friend in concern.

"They've cut his hours, but at least he still has a job. Some of the other men were laid off."

"But Ken is a foreman, and he's been with Bailey Construction for years."

Sally shrugged. "If there isn't any work, that doesn't count."

"I'm really sorry," Dorian faltered.

"I'm sure it won't come to that, but Kenny is a worrier. Especially now that I'm pregnant." Sally mustered a smile. "Our timing wasn't the greatest."

"My grandmother always said babies bring their own luck," Dorian told her soothingly.

Sally laughed. "This one better come loaded with it."

Ken rejoined them, wiping his hands on a paper towel. "Okay, the fire is started. What other little chores do you have for me?"

"You can make us all a drink," Sally said. "Raif will have to catch up when he gets here."

"I wonder what's keeping him," Dorian remarked. "I showered, washed my hair and put on makeup in less time than it's taking him."

"Maybe he had an errand to do on the way home," Sally said. "He was at your house all day."

"You just happened to notice that through your window?" Dorian asked dryly.

Sally grinned. "I had a little trouble with that big orange tree in my front yard, but I managed to see around it."

"Don't bother to have it trimmed. I'll be gone in two weeks."

They were halfway through their gin and tonics before Raif showed up, looking like the virile men featured in advertisements. He was casually dressed in beige linen slacks and a cream-colored silk shirt open at the throat.

"How are you, old buddy?" Ken clasped Raif's shoulder affectionately. "It's about time you spent an evening with us."

"It's good to see you," Raif answered, sidestepping the implied criticism. "How's everything going?"

"Okay, I guess. What have you been doing with yourself since you got back?"

"Nothing special." Raif handed Sally the bottle of wine he was carrying and smiled at both women.

"How nice, but you shouldn't have," Sally chided. Her eyebrows climbed as she read the label. "Imported from France. This is too elegant to serve with hamburgers."

"Save it for a special occasion," Dorian advised.

"This *is* a special occasion," Ken declared. "The four of us together again. It brings back fond memories."

"Where were you so long?" Sally asked Raif, cutting her husband off hastily. "Dorian has been here for half an hour."

"I had a phone call that delayed me," he explained.

From Linda no doubt, Dorian surmised. Or did Raif call *her?* "You're in great demand," she commented lightly.

Ken spared him the necessity of replying. "You're behind the rest of us. What can I fix you?"

"Whatever you're all having." Raif followed him into the house.

"I didn't put Kenny up to that remark, I swear," Sally said when she and Dorian were alone. "I even passed on your warning, but you know how men are. They say anything that pops into their heads."

"It's all right." Dorian sighed. "I suppose we can't ignore the past. We did spend a lot of time together."

"That's why I was hoping it could be the way it used to be. Raif's gotten even better looking," Sally said hopefully.

"Men always do."

"Not like that. He has a kind of lean, adventurous look. I wonder where he's been all these years?"

"Why don't you ask him?"

Although Raif seemed reluctant to talk about himself, Sally was persistent. Under her grilling he opened up and revealed a nomadic life-style. In the intervening years since leaving Summerville, he'd worked in the Middle East, in Africa and most recently in South America.

Ken regarded him with respect. "You've really covered a lot of territory."

Raif grinned. "Some men just can't hang onto a job."

"That's a universal problem," Ken said heavily.

"You must be good at what you do since you kept getting hired," Sally told Raif. She gazed at him curiously. "Exactly what did you do in all those foreign countries?"

"In the early years I built bridges and dams."

He went on to describe the challenge of taming wild rivers and hacking through jungles. Although he didn't say so, it sounded like dangerous work.

"And after that?" Sally prompted.

Raif's generous mouth tightened. "I got into the construction field."

His whole manner showed distaste for the job, in contrast to the quiet pride that was evident when he spoke of his former occupation. What had happened to short-circuit Raif's career, Dorian wondered? Had he been reduced to doing odd jobs to stay afloat? Was that how he learned carpentry and painting and all the rest? Her heart ached for him.

"Hey, we're in the same business," Ken exclaimed.

Raif's constraint was replaced by a smile. "Except that you're working and I'm retired at the moment."

"I might join you any day now," Ken said ruefully.

"You're just borrowing trouble," Sally protested.

"Is there a problem?" Raif asked.

Ken forced a smile. "Not really. Sally's right, I have to stop being so insecure. I'm the kind of guy who wears a belt in addition to suspenders."

"Maybe it would help to talk about it," Raif said slowly.

"If you really want to help, you can keep me company while I put the hamburgers on the grill. I need someone to share the responsibility if they aren't cooked right. Sally won't yell at *you*."

"Stop trying to give the impression that you're henpecked." Sally smiled fondly at her husband.

The evening passed more pleasantly than Dorian had anticipated, even though reminiscences were inevitable. Since she was prepared for the fact by now, they even proved to be fun. Her marriage to Raif held the only painful memories and they skirted around that subject. Darkness fell as they sat at the table laughing and talking after dinner.

"Don't you have an old photo album around somewhere?" Raif asked Sally when they mentioned someone he couldn't remember.

She darted a quick glance at Dorian. "I did have, but I've no idea where it is now."

"It's on the bottom shelf of the bookcase," Ken said helpfully.

Dorian laughed at the chagrined look on Sally's face. "Okay, let's go inside and relive our youth."

"It's scarcely over," Raif objected mildly.

"Certain aspects of it are, thank the Lord," Sally observed. "Do you recall the torture of waiting by the phone for a date for Saturday night?" she asked Dorian.

"I thought the suspense was kind of intriguing," Dorian said.

"Sure, because your only problem was which guy to choose. You had them waiting in line."

"How well I remember." Raif chuckled. "It's a good thing I don't discourage easily. I had a lot of competition."

"They didn't stand a chance after you made your move," Sally said. "None of the high school boys could compete with you."

"Was that my only claim to fame?" Raif asked Dorian quietly.

He knew it wasn't. From the very beginning she'd been drawn to him like a magnet. His youthful physique hadn't filled out to its present, splendid proportions, but when Raif held her in his arms, Dorian ached to belong to him. He was the one who practiced restraint. She would have given him anything.

Sally provided a merciful diversion. Pointing to a picture in the album she said, "There we all are at Ferndale Pond. Remember the fun we had swimming there before old man Richardson bought the property and posted No Trespassing signs?"

"The pond wasn't anywhere near his house," Ken said disgustedly. "He was just a mean old coot."

"Actually, Barnaby Richardson was only in his early fifties back then," Raif said. "We just thought of him as old."

"He was definitely strange," Dorian said. "Nobody knew anything about him except that he was a wealthy recluse. He lived in that big house all alone."

"The only person who has ever been inside it is Lettie O'Toole," Sally said. "She goes there once a week to clean."

"You mean he still lives here?" Dorian exclaimed.

"If you can call solitary confinement living."

The talk drifted to other people and places, and the hours passed swiftly. Dorian became aware of the time when she noticed their host trying to smother a yawn.

"Poor Ken is falling asleep," she said. "We'd better go."

"I didn't mean to break up the party," he apologized. "But construction workers get up early."

"We all have to work tomorrow." Raif stood up and stretched. "Dorian has a full day planned for me, no doubt."

"It's a dirty job, but I offer fringe benefits," she told him.

His eyes kindled. "That sounds provocative."

"I was referring to lunch," she said reprovingly.

Raif laughed. "That's the trouble with the world. You think you're going to get a pony, and someone hands you a shovel instead."

"If that's a criticism of my culinary ability, you can brown bag it tomorrow."

After saying good-night to their hosts, Dorian and Raif continued to joke together lightly as he walked her across the street. His hand clasped her shoulder loosely in a comradely manner that was almost impersonal.

When they reached her front door, the illusion vanished. Dorian was suddenly very much aware of Raif as a man, a physically compelling one. She felt like a schoolgirl again, wondering if he was going to kiss her goodnight.

Fumbling nervously in her purse for the door key she said, "It's so dark. I should have left the porch light on."

"I have a flashlight, if it still works." He drew a key chain out of his pocket. The small flashlight attached to it gave off a feeble glow. "Does that do any good?"

"Yes, here it is." She held up a shiny object. When his hand reached for hers, she jerked it away. "Good night, Raif. I'll see you in the morning." To her complete disgust, she couldn't control the quiver in her voice.

"It's polite to see a lady inside her house before leaving," he commented dryly. "If you'll give me the key, I'll open the door for you."

"That isn't necessary." She stabbed blindly at the lock, unable to find the slot in the darkness.

Raif watched her with a puzzled frown. "What's wrong, Dorian?"

"Nothing, I... it's late and I'm tired."

"Naturally. It must be all of eleven o'clock." His mocking tone faded as he turned her to face him. "We were getting along so well. What did I do to spoil the mood?"

"Nothing," she repeated, holding herself rigid and averting her eyes so he wouldn't guess. The warmth of his hands was adding to her distress.

Raif had always been perceptive where she was concerned. "You thought I intended to kiss you," he said gently.

"Well, I . . . yes," she admitted.

"Would that be so terrible?" His hands moved over her shoulders to circle her throat. A pulse in the small hollow began to throb under his slowly rotating thumb.

She moistened her dry lips. "It wouldn't be a good idea."

He smiled meltingly. "I think it would be a fantastic idea."

For one wild moment Dorian agreed with him. Then she summoned every ounce of willpower, aware of her own vulnerability. If Raif kissed her it wouldn't end there. Not when they both wanted the same thing. He had always been able to reduce her to a mindless mass of desire with one deep kiss, one sensuous caress. But that mustn't be allowed to happen again.

She stepped back and looked at him squarely. "You were right about tonight. We did get along well. But that doesn't change anything. The decision is up to you this time. Either we keep our friendship strictly platonic, or we stop seeing each other."

"I admire your ability to define relationships so precisely." The moonlight highlighted his sardonic expression.

Dorian tensed as Raif closed the small distance between them with catlike swiftness. She retreated until her back was against the door. Then his head dipped, blotting out the light.

Raif's lips trailed across her cheek to the corner of her mouth, but no farther. He raised his head and smiled into her dazzled eyes. "Good night, Dorian. Enjoy the sleep of the righteous."

She watched as he walked unhurriedly across the street and got into his truck. When he waved, aware of her silent scrutiny, she turned quickly and entered the house.

Raif had effectively destroyed the relaxed mood of the evening. Dorian's mind was in turmoil and her body was as taut as a violin string, throbbing with unfulfilled longing. No other man had ever affected her this strongly. Dear God, was she still in love with Raif?

The idea was totally unacceptable. His attraction was entirely physical, she insisted. Maybe she should have gone to bed with him and proved it to herself. But Dorian knew that was a dangerous solution. Raif already dominated her thoughts. If he filled her body as well, he would possess her again.

Perhaps she had scared him off tonight. His parting words were enigmatic. He might not show up tomorrow, now that she'd put an end to his expectations. After all, why should he?

Dorian got undressed wearily, trying to remind herself of her plush office in Los Angeles, and the even more elegant apartment above the Sunset Strip. She'd outgrown Raif. Then why couldn't she seem to forget their torrid nights together? a small voice asked.

Dorian was in the garage early the next morning, working with grim determination. She forced herself not to look up every time a car drove by. Raif wouldn't be back. Besides, this was *her* problem. She hadn't anticipated any help with it, so why expect any? When his truck pulled into the driveway about ten o'clock, her heart soared like a wayward balloon.

"I'm sorry to be so late," he apologized. "I got stuck on the damn phone again."

Her spirits dampened slightly, but she was too happy to see him to quibble. "I thought you weren't coming."

"I told you I'd be here," he chided. "Your trouble is, you don't have any faith in people."

"I've found they usually need an incentive." She tried to make a joke, realizing too late that it was a loaded one.

His mouth curled in a derisive smile. "Maybe I still believe I have prospects." Before she could react he said, "We should finish here by noon. Then I'll take all the junk to the dump so we can begin on the house."

Dorian's apprehensions faded as the day wore on, since Raif seemed to have accepted her ultimatum. She couldn't help being a little piqued at his easy acquiescence, but she knew that was simply vanity.

The garage was finished by noon as Raif had promised, and after lunch they started emptying bedroom closets. That wasn't any easy job. Dorian's throat felt tight as she folded clothing her parents had worn. One dress of her mother's was still scented with her delicate perfume.

Raif kept up a running commentary while he worked, but he paused when he glanced over and noticed her bowed head. Climbing down from the step stool he was using to clear off the top shelves, he came over to Dorian and put his arms around her.

"I know it's hard, honey, but you'll get through this."

She rested her forehead on his chest. "I still can't accept it. Why did they have to die so young?"

Raif stroked her hair tenderly. "Sometimes God gets lonesome and he calls his favorite people home."

"It isn't fair. They have each other, but I don't have anybody," she said in a choked voice.

"You have me," he answered gently.

Dorian felt a measure of peace in Raif's arms. She'd almost forgotten how strong he was. Raif had always been there for her in a crisis. Except for that one traumatic period in their lives. But people made mistakes they regretted. Wasn't it time she gave him another chance?

When she raised her head slowly and gazed up at him, Raif drew a harsh breath. For a moment his arms tightened, molding her body to his hard frame. She could feel the accelerated beat of his heart against her breast, and her own heart began to beat faster. Then his hands gripped her shoulders and moved her away.

"You need a break, and we could both use some fresh air," he said briskly. "Let's go outside and see what we can do about the garden."

"I have a handyman who takes care of it," she answered haltingly.

Dorian was confused and unhappy. Raif seemed to have gotten her message. She couldn't be mistaken about his instant response. Then why this sudden rejection?

"You need a new handyman," he was saying. "Your yard looks neglected."

"Ralph isn't very good," she acknowledged, regaining her poise. "I noticed that the first day I arrived. If I were going to keep the property I'd get someone else, but there's no point in changing now."

"First impressions are important," Raif remarked as he led her to the front door. "Prospective buyers see the outside of the house first. At least we can turn on the sprinklers and do a little pruning."

Dorian had to admit he was right. The front yard did look shabby. Brown patches disfigured the lawn and the rose bushes were covered with withered blooms.

"I'm glad we saved the garden tools," Raif commented. "Turn on the sprinklers while I go and get them."

She clipped off dead blossoms and pulled weeds while he edged the flower beds neatly. It was a glorious day and Dorian was enjoying the sunshine, but she felt guilty.

"I should be inside finishing those closets."

"This is just as important," he assured her, mopping his forehead with a tanned forearm. "Boy, that sun is hot."

"Isn't it, though?" She wiped her upper lip. "I'd like to run through the sprinklers."

"Why don't we?"

"With our clothes on?"

Raif grinned. "It would cause less talk than taking them off. Come on." He took her hand and pulled her to her feet.

Dorian squealed as the cool water hit her heated skin. "It's cold!"

"But refreshing." He gathered her long hair in both hands and drew it to the top of her head so the spray could reach her neck. "This will cool you off."

"I must look a mess," she protested.

"No, you don't. You look like an enchanting water sprite." He ducked his head and playfully licked a drop of water off the tip of her nose.

They frolicked on the lawn like two children, stepping on the sprinkler heads to watch the water bubble between their toes, and sticking their tongues out to catch the spray.

"Something just occurred to me," Dorian called to Raif after a while. "You don't have any clothes to change to."

He shrugged. "I'll dry off in the sun."

"Your shirt maybe, but jeans take forever to dry."

"Don't worry about it, my truck has leather seats. A little dampness won't hurt them."

"I have an idea. You can wear a pair of Dad's slacks while I throw your jeans in the dryer. I'll go see what I can find that will fit you."

Raif raised one eyebrow. "I take it playtime is over?"

"You guessed right." Dorian turned off the sprinklers and walked toward the kitchen entrance. "We've wasted enough time."

He caught up with her and held the door open, following her inside. "Do you really consider it wasted?"

"No, it was fun," she answered softly.

He stroked the wet hair off her forehead. "I think you need more fun in your life."

The touch of his long fingers sent a quiver down her spine. But Dorian didn't want to risk another rejection. Uttering a tentative laugh, she pulled at her sodden T-shirt.

"You're already a corrupting influence. What would my business associates say if they saw me like this?"

When Raif's eyes swept over her and began to glow like twin emeralds, Dorian realized it was obvious she wasn't wearing a bra. The wet T-shirt revealed not only the contours of her breasts, but her nipples as well. The rose-colored points were clearly defined under the thin white fabric.

She quickly crossed her arms over her chest, but he took her wrists and held her arms apart. "They'd be very lucky if they had a chance to see you like this." His voice was husky.

"Raif, please," she whispered, starting to tremble.

"You always did have the most beautiful breasts I've ever seen." He released her wrists, but his hands moved to her waist, sliding under the hem of her shirt and trailing up her sides.

She grabbed ineffectually at his arms. "Stop it, Raif," she said weakly.

"Do you really want me to?" he murmured.

His hands were cupping her breasts now, and his fingertips stroked each curled rosette. A shower of golden sparks shot through her body, setting it on fire. She clutched at his shoulders, unable to reply, although her answer was evident.

He drew her close and buried his face in her neck. "I've missed you, angel."

His mouth closed over hers with a hunger that fueled Dorian's own passion. All reservations were swept aside by Raif's mouth, his hands, the molten sensation of his taut body making her aware of his power.

She twined her fingers through his hair, uttering incoherent little cries of pleasure as his tongue plundered her mouth. Their bodies moved together restlessly, escalating an urgency neither could deny.

Suddenly the doorbell shrilled, yanking them down from the heights. They stared at each other in confusion, finding it difficult to make the transition to reality. When footsteps sounded at the side of the house, Dorian moved away from Raif and tried to control the excitement still raging through her veins.

"Hello! Is anybody home?" Linda's voice preceded her a moment before she appeared outside the screen door. "I saw Raif's truck in the driveway so I knew you must be around somewhere. Isn't your doorbell working?"

Once again Linda was perfectly groomed. Dorian folded her arms over her revealing shirtfront and mumbled something unintelligible.

"May I come in?" Linda didn't wait for an answer. After she'd entered the kitchen and taken a clearer look at them, her jaw dropped. "Good grief, what happened to you two?"

"We were adjusting the sprinklers," Raif answered smoothly. He had recovered his aplomb.

"Dorian looks half-drowned." Linda inspected her incredulously.

"Thanks for sharing that with me," Dorian snapped. "I wasn't expecting company," she added pointedly.

"This is a business call. I brought some people to see your house."

"I haven't even put it on the market yet," Dorian exclaimed.

"I know, but a couple dropped by my office looking for a home in this neighborhood, and I thought of you right away. When I described your house to them, they were very interested. Can I show them around? They're outside in the car."

"That's unfortunate, because this isn't a convenient time." Keeping her arms crossed, Dorian hunched her shoulders and reached up awkwardly to brush a strand of sodden hair off her cheek. "In the future I'd appreciate it if you'd phone ahead for an appointment."

"I will, I promise. But as long as they're already here, couldn't we take a quick peek?" Linda wheedled.

A swift glance told Raif how uncomfortable Dorian was. "I think Dorian would prefer to get cleaned up first," he told Linda.

"We won't bother her. I'll tell my clients they can't go into your bedroom," she assured Dorian. "If they're as interested as I think, they'll be willing to come back."

Dorian couldn't believe the woman's persistence. "Isn't it customary for realtors to check out a property first?" she asked acidly. "You've never been inside this house. You don't even know the floor plan."

Linda was only stumped for a moment. "Raif can show us around. You wouldn't mind, would you?" She gazed at him appealingly.

He hesitated. "Well, if it's all right with Dorian."

Dorian was furious with both of them, but her anger at Raif was mixed with bitterness. A few moments ago he'd been making passionate love to her, but that wasn't as important as helping Linda make a sale. What did that say about his priorities?

"You won't even know we're here," Linda promised Dorian, taking her permission for granted. "I'll go and get my clients."

After she'd left, Raif said, "You can start getting cleaned up. I'll keep them out of your hair."

It was only a figure of speech, but Dorian was reminded of her bedraggled appearance. "I don't know what I'd do without you," she said coldly. "Just be sure to lock the front door when you leave."

He couldn't fail to understand her message, but Dorian stayed in the shower for a long time to be certain Raif had gone. An unnecessary precaution, no doubt. He and Linda were probably out celebrating, she thought grimly.

Underneath her burning anger was a feeling of betrayal. How could Raif have kissed her like that without any deeper emotion being involved? Was passion all he felt? Evidently. His loyalties were clearly with Linda.

Dorian shuddered when she pictured what would have happened without that interruption. At least she hadn't let Raif make love to her. How easily he'd gotten her to trust him again. It was a sobering reminder for the future. Not that they had one together. Her last ties to Summerville would be severed soon, and then she never wanted to see Raif Dangerfield again.

* * *

Dorian couldn't believe her eyes when Raif's truck rattled into her driveway the next morning. Did he really think he could juggle Linda and her, too? She'd disabuse him of *that* notion in a hurry!

Flinging open the door, she scowled fiercely. "What are you doing here again?"

He gazed back at her enigmatically. "I don't like to leave things unfinished."

"I don't need your help anymore," she said tautly. "You did enough yesterday."

"Would you please tell me what's bothering you? It wasn't *my* fault Linda chose to drop in unannounced. Believe me, I regretted the intrusion more than you did." His mouth twisted wryly.

How could he be such a hypocrite? "You certainly offered her your services rapidly enough!"

"Is that what you're angry about? I thought I was doing you a favor."

"Me, or Linda?" she asked scornfully.

Raif sighed. "I know you're anxious to sell the house. I thought the only reason you didn't want to let those people in was because you weren't exactly presentable. That's why I agreed to do it for you."

"She could have brought them back some other time," Dorian said stubbornly.

"True, but if they were really interested, you would have had a quick sale."

"The two of you can't wait to get me out of town," she said childishly.

"Do you really believe that, Dorian? Is that the reason I spend all day here hauling boxes and cleaning cobwebs out of dark corners?"

Her eyes wavered before his steady gaze. When he put it that way, her accusation sounded mean-spirited. But whose side was Raif on? She no longer trusted his motives.

He watched uncertainty cloud her face. "I know you're under stress right now," he said quietly. "You have an unenviable job ahead of you. I thought I could help, but if I'm only adding to your troubles, I'll leave you alone."

Dorian's anger was replaced by shame. Raif didn't deserve the abuse she was constantly subjecting him to. For whatever reason, he'd been a great help to her. She had no right to expect more.

"Would you like to come inside for a cup of coffee?" She forced a smile to hide the fear that he might refuse. "If we stand out here much longer, Sally will be over to find out what's going on."

His warm smile told her she was forgiven. "I'd love a cup of coffee. And I wouldn't mind a doughnut if you have one lying around."

With this resumption of their former friendly relations, Dorian vowed not to overreact again. Especially not over Linda, however much she might deplore Raif's taste.

While they were sitting at the kitchen table drinking coffee, Raif remarked, "I spoke to Carrie about your idea for a teen hangout, and she thought it was a winner. She's anxious to meet you and get your input."

In the spirit of atonement Dorian said, "Let's start in the kitchen this morning. We can pack up a lot of this stuff and take it to the Center this afternoon."

"Won't you need to use it while you're here?"

"Only a small part. There's enough to stock an army mess hall."

Dorian's assessment was accurate. They spent most of the day packing away dishes, glassware and various gadgets. In the afternoon Raif loaded the cartons designated for the Center onto his truck, and Dorian went with him to deliver them.

The former nursery school was a one-story structure built on a large lot. The small building sparkled under a coat of white paint, and the shutters were lacquered a cheery green.

Inside was a long room dominated at one end by a large television set. The wall facing the backyard was lined with windows that should have filled the room with sunshine. But most of the blinds were drawn for the benefit of a handful of people grouped around the TV set.

Dorian was appalled. Was this what they did all day? None of them were in wheelchairs or had any obvious disabilities. Before she could question Raif, a woman approached from the opposite end of the room.

She had dark hair highlighted by a dramatic streak of white at one temple. Dorian couldn't tell if it was natural or bleached. The woman was somewhere in her fifties, she judged, very attractive with a still-trim figure.

"This is Carrie Madison," Raif informed Dorian, then introduced her to the other woman.

"I've been dying to meet you," Carrie told Dorian. "Raif said such flattering things about you, and I thought your idea was very exciting."

"It was only a suggestion. I don't know if it's practical." Dorian was doubtful, now that she'd seen some of the Center's habitués.

"That's probably what the early cavemen said about the wheel," Raif commented.

When a torrent of sibilant sounds came from the group around the TV set, Carrie made a rueful face. "Let's go in the kitchen where we can talk without incurring the wrath of the couch potatoes."

The kitchen was rather bare, but it had a table and four chairs. Dorian and Raif sat at the table while Carrie heated water for tea.

"When a certain kind donor gave us that television set I was as thrilled as the others." The older woman sighed. "But it's proved to be a mixed blessing."

Had Raif given it to the Center, Dorian wondered? The set looked new, and a screen that large had to have been expensive. Judging by Raif's ancient truck and certain other indications, he must be on a tight budget, but it would be just like him to scrimp on himself to help others. He wouldn't even want to be known as the donor, which would also be like him.

After a look at her pensive face, Raif said swiftly, "Dorian's plan should cure their addiction. Tell Carrie how we can turn this place around," he urged.

"It's really ideal for the purpose," Dorian said. "You could erect a basketball hoop in the backyard, and maybe string up a badminton net. There's plenty of room out there."

"A barbecue would be nice, too, and some picnic tables and benches," Raif contributed.

"The kids won't be eating here," Dorian reminded him.

"You never know. Your extended family idea could lead to potluck dinners now and then."

"I hate to sound a negative note, but we don't have money for all the equipment you're talking about," Carrie lamented.

"It wouldn't take much," Raif answered.

Carrie looked dubious. "We barely manage to pay the rent and utilities. Not much is left over after that. We try to keep the dues low because most of the members are on a fixed income."

"Well then, you'll just have to raise the money from outside sources," Dorian decided.

"How?"

"There are dozens of ways—baby-sitting, bake sales, a raffle. The first thing you have to do, though, is unplug that TV set. This has to be a team effort to succeed."

Carrie looked at her admiringly. "This girl is a dynamo, Raif. Isn't there any way we can keep her around?"

"I tried that, but it didn't work," he said softly.

Dorian avoided his eyes. "Get a pencil and paper, Carrie," she said briskly. "We should start making some notes."

Dorian was filled with animation when she and Raif left the Center some time later. "I think we can really make this project work," she declared.

He gazed at her with fond indulgence. "Thanks to your driving force. Carrie's right. You *are* a dynamo."

"She's not too slow moving herself. I can't understand what she's doing with all those stodgy old people. She must be years younger than they."

Raif shrugged. "You can't tell about women. Carrie is probably older than she looks."

"What do you know about her?"

"Not a great deal. She was widowed a few years ago, and I don't think she had any relatives in Summerville. That's probably why she's so involved in the Center."

"Well, I hope for her sake we can make it more stimulating."

"It was good of you to take the time." Raif squeezed Dorian's hand. "As a token of appreciation, I'd like to make dinner for you at my house tomorrow night."

She slanted a provocative glance at him. "That sounds lovely, but I'm not doing anything tonight either."

He hesitated. "Tomorrow would really be better."

"No problem. Tomorrow will be fine." Dorian smiled brightly.

She refused to speculate about Raif's plans for the evening—not that it would take much imagination. But this time she intended to act like an adult. Dorian smiled mirthlessly. That's the way Raif would be acting.

Chapter Four

Dorian drove herself to Raif's house the next night. He had offered to pick her up, but she convinced him there was no need. She was trying very hard to keep their relationship casual, and it would seem less like a date if he didn't call for her. Not that she told him that, of course.

"I know what the problem is. You don't want to be seen riding in my old truck." Raif was smiling, but his eyes were watchful.

Dorian didn't bother to refute the accusation, since she assumed he was joking. "I've been wondering about that. Why did you buy a truck instead of a car?"

He shrugged. "I ran across a fellow who needed money, and I needed wheels."

Meaning the truck was cheap, Dorian deduced. She changed the subject. "Can I bring something for dinner tonight?"

"Just an appetite." He looked at his watch. "I'm going to leave now. I have a few things to pick up at the market."

Dorian had difficulty deciding what to wear that evening. She hadn't brought anything fancy, although it wouldn't be appropriate anyhow. Still, she wanted to look nice as a courtesy to her host. She finally decided on a simple blue linen sheath and high-heeled white sandals. It would be the first time Raif had seen her dressed decently.

After brushing her hair until it floated around her face like a dark golden cloud, she applied makeup. Blue eyeshadow to accentuate the color of her eyes, and mascara on her long thick lashes. She outlined her mouth with a deep coral lipstick, then filled in with a lighter shade. Just a touch of blush on her high cheekbones gave a delicate flush to her clear skin.

This was the way she dressed to go out in L.A., Dorian assured herself. She wasn't going to any special lengths. One thing she had to admit, however. Not in a long time had she experienced this pleasurable feeling of anticipation for an evening.

Raif's reception was worth all the pains she'd taken. His eyes gleamed as they swept over her glamorous face and curved figure.

"You look sensational," he exclaimed.

"You're not too shabby yourself," she answered honestly.

He had changed to white linen slacks and a black silk shirt. The sleeves were partially rolled up, exposing the muscular forearms she'd had occasion to admire before.

Dorian sniffed at the appetizing aroma coming from the kitchen. "Something smells delicious. What are we having for dinner?"

"Roast chicken with saffron rice. I wanted to show you how easy it is. After working all day you can still whip up something healthy without spending hours in the process."

"I thought I was invited for dinner, not a lecture," Dorian complained.

"This is only the beginning. I show slides on nutrition later." He grinned mischievously.

"At least you haven't become a teetotaler. I think I'll have a double martini."

"It won't help to fall asleep," he teased. "I'll just wake you up and show them again."

Dorian sighed theatrically. "I should have known you had an ulterior motive in asking me here."

"I hoped you wouldn't guess." Something flickered in Raif's eyes, although his voice was joking.

"I still can't picture you as a chef. I always thought you were helpless in the kitchen."

"Perhaps that was the trouble with us. We had preconceived images of each other." Before Dorian could take offense, Raif's set expression lightened. "I must admit that learning to cook was a survival instinct. When you're in the African bush or a desert in the Middle East, you'd better know how to get a meal together."

"Is that what turned you on to natural foods?"

"Some of it was quite exotic."

"Like what?"

He grinned. "Do you really want to know?"

"Maybe not."

"Good thinking. I want you to enjoy your dinner."

Dorian enjoyed more than merely his cooking. The entire evening was delightful. They laughed and talked easily together, with no troubling undercurrents.

After dinner they had coffee in the living room and continued their conversation without a pause. Dorian hadn't realized how much she'd missed being with a man she could actually talk to. Raif seemed genuinely interested in her ideas and opinions, unlike the men she was accustomed to, who mostly wanted something different. Impulsively, she told him that.

"You're a beautiful woman," he answered. "Surely you aren't surprised when men want to make love to you."

"I might be flattered if their passion sprang from something more than excess hormones," she replied tartly.

Raif's eyes glinted with amusement. "That's the difference between males and females. Men can enjoy sex as a pleasant diversion, whereas women require a declaration of love first."

"Not necessarily love, but at least there should be some affectionate caring."

"I agree wholeheartedly." He slanted her an oblique look. "I find it hard to believe you haven't had a lot of men fall in love with you during these years. In fact, I'm surprised you didn't remarry."

"I could say the same about you."

He smiled. "I'm not as desirable as you."

"I wouldn't say that." She inspected his rugged face and the splendid proportions of his long, relaxed body. "I'm sure you've attracted more than your share of willing women."

"Then what do you suppose we're waiting for?" he asked in a teasing voice.

"Perhaps we ruined each other for anyone else," she answered just as jokingly.

Raif's face sobered as he took her hand. "I'm sorry you were hurt, but our marriage was the best thing that ever happened to me. I'm a more caring person because of you."

"That's a nice thing to say," she replied softly.

"It's true." The pressure of his hand increased. "I want to talk to you about something."

Before he could continue, the telephone rang. Raif went to answer it, leaving Dorian in a state of mental turmoil. Was he going to suggest they start over? Was that the real reason he asked her here tonight? Raif had made his feelings clear from their first meeting, even if they were only physical. The attraction between them was still there; it was useless to pretend differently.

But suppose it was more than that? What would her answer be? She'd have to be crazy to agree. They were completely changed people now; they disagreed on so many things. Yet even as she faced irrefutable facts, a tremulous happiness filled Dorian. They were both too mature to rush into anything, but if they talked things out and resolved their differences, anything was possible.

Raif had picked up the wall phone in the kitchen, which was only a few steps from the living room in the compact little house. Although Dorian didn't want to eavesdrop, she couldn't help hearing his end of the conversation.

Raif's voice was filled with urgency. "Finally! Every time the phone rang I expected it to be you." After a pause, "You could have found a minute to call. That isn't too unreasonable. You must have known I was waiting to hear from you."

Dorian's rosy glow began to evaporate as she listened openly now. The caller was someone Raif was very involved with. Those were the kind of recriminations lovers hurled at each other.

"I offered to meet you and talk about any problems," he was saying. "I realize you need time, but I'm tired of waiting." He became impatient at the answer he received. "I'm not going to give up! You must know how much this means to me."

Dorian stood abruptly and went to turn up the stereo so she wouldn't have to listen to Raif's pleas. When she jumped to a conclusion, it was a record-breaking leap! Raif didn't want to resume their relationship, he was about to tell her he'd found someone to take her place.

Bitter laughter constricted Dorian's throat. Did he intend to ask for her blessing? At least she'd had time to prepare herself. As Raif rejoined her, she pinned a bright smile on her face.

"Sorry to take so long," he apologized. "But I've been waiting for that phone call."

"It's quite all right. We're all slaves to the telephone," Dorian replied calmly.

"A necessary evil," he agreed. "Can I get you more coffee?"

"No thanks, I have to be running along."

"It's still early," he protested.

"I don't want to wear out my welcome."

"You couldn't do that." He smiled.

"The time to leave is while you still feel that way," she answered lightly. "Good night, Raif. Thanks for a delicious dinner."

"I hope you'll come again soon." He walked her to her car and opened the door. "I'll see you in the morning."

"Not tomorrow," she said quickly, sliding into the driver's seat. "I've decided to take the day off."

"That's a good idea. You've been working too hard. What do you plan to do?"

"I haven't decided yet." She started the motor. "Maybe I'll go shopping with Sally. You know that old saying— when the going gets tough, the tough go shopping."

His expression was gentle. "I realize it's rough for you now, but better times are coming."

"I'm not counting on it. I stopped believing in fairy tales a long time ago." With a wave of her hand, Dorian drove away.

Raif stared at the glowing taillights with narrowed eyes. When they disappeared around the corner he went back into the house.

Dorian slept late the next morning, an unaccustomed luxury. The hour spent reading the morning paper was another indulgence, as was dawdling over a second cup of coffee.

She hadn't really expected to take the day off. That was only an excuse to keep Raif away without admitting that his presence was becoming disturbing. But a free day began to sound more and more appealing. She needed to get out of the house.

In the late morning Dorian telephoned Sally. After a little preliminary chitchat she asked, "How would you like to have lunch at The Oaken Bucket and do some shopping afterward?"

"It sounds heavenly, but I can't," Sally replied regretfully. "The repair man is coming to see if he can coax a few more months out of my ancient washing machine."

"What time will he be there?"

"Only God and the dispatcher know, and they don't share the information with mere mortals."

"Isn't that the truth? Men never consider a woman's time is important. It seems a shame to wait home all afternoon, though. Couldn't you leave the key with a neighbor and pin a note on the door?"

"No, I have to be here. A couple of our other appliances are making death rattles. Maybe he can apply first aid to them before they become terminal.'' Sally sighed. ''You'd better go without me. I can't afford to let myself be tempted, anyway. The repair men will be wearing my new fall clothes.''

''They'll look terrible in short skirts,'' Dorian consoled her.

Without Sally, Dorian was left at loose ends. She had other friends in Summerville, but no one she felt like contacting, and the suggested shopping trip was solely for recreation. She didn't need to buy anything.

On an impulse, Dorian drove to the Senior Citizen's Center. Carrie Madison was an interesting woman she'd like to know better. If she was free, Carrie would be a satisfactory substitute for Sally.

Dorian was surprised at the activity around the Center. She even had trouble finding a place to park. A large banner draped over the door told her the reason. It read Cake Sale Today Only.

People were standing and talking in little groups around the entrance, exchanging greetings with friends entering or leaving the small building. All the ones coming out were carrying plastic-covered paper plates containing baked goods.

The atmosphere inside was a far cry from its former somnolence. Card tables were set up down the middle of the long room, and people were clustered around them, selecting from a variety of cakes and cookies. Ladies in frilly aprons filled orders and directed customers to a table near the front door where Carrie took their money.

Her face lit up when she saw Dorian. ''Isn't this a wonderful turnout?''

''Unbelievable! How did you organize this thing so fast?''

"I just acted on your idea." Carrie made change for a ten-dollar bill. "There you are, Mrs. Rawlings. Enjoy your coconut cake."

When she had her attention again, Dorian said, "I'm really impressed. I thought you'd hold meetings first and appoint committees."

Carrie grinned. "We didn't realize we were supposed to."

"Are you making fun of me?" Dorian demanded.

"I wouldn't dream of it." Carrie counted out change for a customer. "You're going to love those brownies," she assured the woman. "People would kill for Hannah's recipe."

As more customers lined up, Dorian said, "You're busy. I'll stop by some other time."

"Don't go," Carrie urged. "I need a break. I'll get Muriel to take over for me and we can go out in the yard and talk."

The backyard was peaceful in comparison to the din inside. They strolled to the back fence where roses bloomed in wild profusion, perfuming the air.

"Your first venture is certainly a winner," Dorian commented. "You might think about making it a regular event."

"It could be just a novelty," Carrie said doubtfully. "People are enjoying getting together."

"I noticed that. You could have increased your profits if you'd sold coffee, and slices of cake to eat here."

"*Now* you tell me."

"It doesn't matter. You're a big success, anyway."

"A qualified one," Carrie answered ruefully. "I made an estimate of our profits before the sale began. Even if we sell out completely, we won't be anywhere near our goal."

"It's a beginning. There are lots of other ways to raise money."

"They'll all take longer than this. I like your idea of a raffle, but we'd have to find some really attractive prizes and allow plenty of time to print and sell tickets. The whole project would take a month at the very least."

"That isn't very long."

"I suppose you're right, but I'm so anxious to get the youth center started. All the parents I've spoken to have been really enthusiastic. I'd hate to think it might take us a year to get off the ground."

"You're being too pessimistic," Dorian protested. "We aren't talking about a huge sum of money."

"Not to some people. Too bad the haves aren't as generous as the have nots. Would you believe Raif actually offered to give us the cash we need?"

Dorian couldn't help shaking her head. "I'm not surprised."

"Of course I refused. I know he can't afford it, but wasn't that darling of him?"

"Adorable," Dorian answered dryly.

"Don't tell him I told you. He didn't want anyone to know. I wouldn't have mentioned it, but I thought he might have discussed it with you. I know he values your opinion."

"I think you've gotten the wrong impression," Dorian said carefully. "I hadn't seen or heard from Raif in years until I returned to Summerville a few days ago."

"Real friendships are like that," Carrie remarked with an innocent expression. "You can pick up where you left off, no matter how long it's been."

A friendship maybe, not a romance, Dorian thought somberly. It wasn't a subject she wanted to discuss.

Carrie sensed that and didn't pursue the topic. "I wish we could find some benefactors like Raif who can afford to be generous." Before Dorian could answer, one of the women in an apron waved frantically from the back door. "I'd better get back," Carrie said. "It looks as if we have a crisis."

Dorian walked alongside her with a thoughtful expression on her face. "You may have hit on the solution to your problem."

"I'd be delighted to hear it."

"Well, look at it this way. You'll be providing a community service, so why shouldn't the community do its part?"

Carrie raised her eyebrows. "I'm dedicated, but I can't say I relish the thought of going door-to-door with a tin cup."

"Think big," Dorian advised crisply. "I'm talking about corporate contributions."

"You mean banks and department stores?"

"Why not? It would be good public relations for them."

Carrie paused, staring at Dorian with mixed emotions. "I wouldn't know how to begin," she said uncertainly. "I'm not good at asking for favors."

"Don't think of it that way. The benefits would be mutual. You could be all set up in a month."

Excitement replaced doubt as Carrie said, "I just became convinced. Will you go with me?"

"You don't need me. You're very competent."

"I've never attempted anything like this. Just go with me to one or two places," Carrie pleaded. "I can talk to ordinary people, but the thought of executives intimidates me."

Dorian smiled. "You'd be surprised at how ordinary some executives can be."

"You know what I mean."

"Sure. Rich men don't scare you, but a man with a title does," Dorian teased.

"I haven't had any experience with rich men, either. There aren't too many in Summerville."

"Carrie, we need you!" The woman had appeared in the doorway again, looking harassed. "Mrs. Biedermeier wants to buy half a cake. I told her we couldn't do that, but she's making a big fuss. Maybe you can talk to her."

"I really have to get back," Carrie said to Dorian.

"What time will this thing be over?" Dorian asked.

"Sales are so brisk that I'd say we'll be sold out by the middle of the afternoon."

"Okay, I'll be back to pick you up around three."

"What for?" Carrie asked blankly.

"The banks will be getting ready to close, so we'll begin with a couple of stores."

"You want to start *today?*"

"I'm free all day," Dorian answered calmly. "If you'd rather wait till some other time and go by yourself, it's all right with me."

"That's coercion," Carrie said plaintively.

"Think of it as motivation." Dorian chuckled. "To show you I'm not all bad, I'll buy the other half of Mrs. Biedermeier's cake."

After leaving the Center, Dorian made the rounds of the local real estate offices to list her house for sale. She had put it off through a combination of lethargy and a reluctance to take such a final step. But time was passing, and she couldn't afford to indulge in sentiment any longer.

After her business was taken care of she stopped by the drugstore and the hardware shop for a few necessary items. As she went from place to place in the small town, Dorian wondered if she might bump into Raif. Not that she wanted to. Finding out he was involved with someone was the best thing that could have happened to both of them.

To get her mind off Raif, Dorian began to make up a mental list of prospective donors to the Center. Marten's Department Store would almost certainly make a contribution, and the local supermarket should pledge something, but how much? Trudging all over town promised to be a drag. It would be ideal if they could get one person to underwrite the whole project. It wasn't that costly.

Gradually an idea began to take root, germinated from a remark of Carrie's. It was a wild notion with nearly no chance of success, but unfavorable odds had never daunted Dorian. If nothing else, she might get to satisfy a curiosity that went back many years.

The bake sale was over, and the members were cleaning up when Dorian returned to the Center. Carrie was waiting for her with a noticeable lack of enthusiasm.

"I can't believe I let you talk me into this," she said.

"Your cake sale was a success, wasn't it? Trust me," Dorian advised.

"I once bought a second-hand car from a man who used those same words," Carrie remarked as she got into the passenger seat of Dorian's car. "As soon as the warranty ran out, the only thing that worked was the horn."

"I'm going to give you back your faith in human nature," Dorian soothed.

They chatted about the bake sale, the profits, and how all the members had pitched in. Carrie wasn't paying attention to Dorian's driving, but when they reached the outskirts of town she looked around with a puzzled frown.

"Where are we going?" she asked.

"I thought we'd drop in on Barnaby Richardson."

"The recluse?" Carrie's eyes widened. "What on earth for?"

"To give him a chance to fund the Center's youth group."

"You must be out of your mind! He hates people."

"He doesn't have to join. All we want is his money."

"What makes you think he'd give us any? He hasn't contributed to anything that I've ever heard of."

"Maybe nobody ever asked him."

"This is insane," Carrie wailed. "The man might be a lunatic. What other reason could he have for cutting himself off from the world? He's apt to run us off with a shotgun!"

"I doubt that. You're letting your imagination run away with you," Dorian chided. "The worst that could happen is that he might be a little rude."

"Like chasing us with a butcher knife?"

"You're ridiculous," Dorian said briskly as she drove onto a paved courtyard in front of a stately, two-story brick house. "Barnaby Richardson may be a little eccentric, but that doesn't mean he's an ax murderer."

"His choice of lethal weapons doesn't interest me," Carrie muttered as she reluctantly followed Dorian to the front door.

The deep silence was rather eerie. An occasional bird chirped, but the big house was as quiet as a tomb. No one answered when Dorian repeatedly rang the doorbell.

"Nobody's home," Carrie said. "Let's go."

"He should be around here somewhere."

"Maybe this is his way of telling us he doesn't want company. I'm in favor of respecting his wishes."

A man came around the corner of the house, so silently that they didn't hear his footsteps. By his side was a huge black dog that didn't look friendly. Its fathomless expression matched that of its master's.

"Were you looking for someone?" the man asked in a deep voice.

Dorian and Carrie whirled around, then gasped. The man was carrying an ax! He would have looked formidable enough without it. His dark eyes were piercing in a craggy face surmounted by silvery hair, and his lanky frame was as hard-muscled as a cowboy's. The resemblance was accentuated by worn jeans and a denim shirt that spanned his broad chest.

When the two women were incapable of speech he frowned. "Are you lost? In case you didn't notice, this is private property."

"I hope you'll excuse us. We shouldn't have... That is, we must have taken a wrong turn," Carrie babbled. "If you'll just let us leave, we won't bother you again."

As she started to edge gingerly past the dog, the man moved to block her way. "Just a minute. Is anything wrong? You seem upset."

"I'll be fine as soon as I get out of here. I mean, I told my friend we shouldn't bother you," Carrie said hastily.

"You came to see me?" The admission seemed to amaze him.

"I'm really sorry we disturbed you. It was all my fault." Dorian felt she should take responsibility for her ill-advised idea.

"You aren't disturbing me." He lifted the heavy ax and rested it on his shoulder. "Come inside and you can tell me why you're here."

"No!" both women chorused explosively, shrinking back against the door.

His face hardened into stern lines. "Did you come here on a dare? You seem rather mature to be playing childish games."

"It was nothing like that, Mr. Richardson," Dorian said earnestly.

"So you do know who I am." His voice was ominous.

"Yes, but we had a valid reason for coming. At least I thought it was valid. If I made a mistake we'll leave. You don't have to get violent."

He stared at her in disbelief. "Are you sure you're all right?" As he noticed the horrified way their eyes kept swiveling to the ax, Barnaby Richardson began to chuckle. Tossing it onto the grass he said, "I'm afraid we're all victims of a misunderstanding. I was chopping wood out back when I heard the doorbell. Contrary to what you obviously believe, I'm not a dangerous psychopath."

Carrie's cheeks flushed. "We didn't think that."

"Yes, we did." Dorian sighed. "Can you forgive us, Mr. Richardson?"

"I'll consider it, if you'll tell me who you are and what this is all about."

Carrie introduced Dorian and herself. "I live in Summerville, but Dorian is only visiting," she said in an attempt at small talk.

"I left town shortly after you moved here." Dorian added her bit.

He looked at her appraisingly. "You must have been a teenager then."

"I was. My friends and I used to swim on this property before you bought it."

"And chased you off," he finished for her. His smile held a tinge of sadness. "No wonder you have such an unflattering opinion of me."

"That was a long time ago. I'm sure you had your reasons," Dorian answered politely.

A shadow passed over his face, but his voice was light. "I'd like to prove I've mellowed since then. Won't you come inside for a drink or a cup of tea?" When they hesitated, his eyes began to twinkle. "I'll leave the front door open so you can make a quick dash for your car if you feel the need. Will that make you feel more secure?"

Carrie smiled. "That won't be necessary, Mr. Richardson. We'd love a cup of tea, wouldn't we, Dorian?"

After Dorian agreed, he said, "Splendid. And please call me Barnaby."

Both women looked around the house with undisguised curiosity. They had half expected to find dark, cobweb-festooned rooms, but nothing could have been farther from the reality.

A central hall was flanked on the right by a beautifully furnished living room, and on the left by a formal dining room. They followed their host down the hall to a large kitchen and breakfast room combined. A round table placed in a bay of sparkling clean windows looked out on a garden in full bloom.

"This is lovely!" Carrie exclaimed.

Barnaby hid his amusement at their transparent surprise. "I can't take the credit. A local woman keeps the place up."

"Can I help?" Carrie asked as he filled a kettle with water.

"You're a guest." He smiled. "My first in a very long time."

Dorian was puzzled when he began to fill a plate with cookies from the kind of box bakeries use. Where had he gotten them if he never went into town? For that matter, where did he buy his food and the other necessities of daily life?

Carrie was giving Barnaby her full attention. "This is such a beautiful house. I should think you'd have a lot of company," she remarked with apparent innocence.

"I've built up a reputation for being inhospitable," he answered dryly. "You've demonstrated how wary people are of me."

"That's only because you haven't given them a chance to know you," she protested. "Summerville is a very friendly town. I had only lived here a few years when my husband died, but everyone was simply wonderful to me. I don't know what I would have done without them."

"People cope in different ways." Barnaby's expression was sober as he poured the tea. "After my wife died I couldn't bear to be with anyone."

"Was that when you moved here?" Dorian asked.

He nodded. "I needed to get away from anything that reminded me of them."

"Them?" Carrie asked in a hushed voice.

Barnaby stared out the window at a distant vision. "My wife and daughter drowned in a lake in Northern California."

"I'm so sorry," Carrie whispered.

"Melanie, our only child, got a cramp in deep water," he continued in a toneless voice. "Isobel tried to rescue her, but she wasn't a strong swimmer. They both drowned before anyone could reach them."

"What a devastating loss," Dorian murmured.

"My whole life fell apart. I bought this place because it was isolated and I could be alone with my grief."

"No wonder you didn't want us to swim in your pond," Dorian said slowly.

"It brought everything back, all the memories I was running away from."

"But you can talk about it now?" Carrie asked tentatively.

"Time has a merciful way of healing even the deepest wounds," he said simply. "I'll never forget my wife and daughter, but at least now I dwell on our happy times together."

"Then why haven't you taken up your life again?" Carrie asked. "Why do you stay in this big place all alone?"

"I've gotten used to it, and I like the spaciousness. Besides, I'm not alone." He patted the big dog that had followed them indoors. "I have Toby here."

"He can't carry on much of a conversation," Carrie observed.

"Neither can a lot of people." Barnaby grinned. "Present company excluded, of course."

"You seem like such an intelligent man," Carrie persisted. "Doesn't it bother you not to know what's going on in the world?"

"I keep reasonably well informed through the miracle of modern technology—television, radio, books and newspapers."

Dorian asked the question that had been bothering her. "Where do you get necessities, ordinary things like toothpaste and paper towels?"

"I drive to Larkin." He named the next town after Summerville.

Carrie looked at him incredulously. "You're only three miles from town. Why would you go somewhere else to shop?"

He shrugged. "I've found it's worth the trip. Nobody stares at me or scuttles away as if I'm contagious. My reputation precedes me here. In Larkin I'm just another customer."

"You poor man," Carrie exclaimed indignantly. "How can people be so cruel?"

"You just told me how wonderful they are."

"Not all of them, unfortunately, but I'll put a stop to that!"

"What do you plan to do?" His expression changed as he gazed at her pretty, flushed face. "Offer me an escort around town?"

"I'd be happy to. As soon as people got to know you the way we have, they'd be ashamed of their ridiculous prejudices."

After a comprehensive glance at them, Dorian stood up and asked casually, "Would you mind if I strolled over to the pond while you two are finishing your tea? I'd sort of like to recapture my youth."

Barnaby smiled. "You don't have to go back very far."

"It seems a long time ago." She sighed.

"Do you want me to come with you?" Carrie tried to hide her reluctance.

"No, I'd prefer to go alone."

Toby followed Dorian to the door. When they were outside she patted his head. "Smart dog. I'm not the only one who can tell when three's a crowd."

She wandered through sweet-smelling meadows, reflecting on the amazing events of the afternoon. Poor Barnaby, going through such trauma alone. She felt guilty for joining the rest in judging him harshly, but no one could have guessed his tragic secret. She had a hunch life would be a lot brighter for him now, though. What a stroke of luck that she'd brought Carrie here today. The attraction between the older couple was very promising.

Dorian flopped down in the tall grass and closed her eyes. "Why is it I can better the life of every living creature except myself?" she muttered.

Toby pawed at her shoulder and whined. She opened her eyes to see his huge head poised over hers.

"Okay, so I didn't get around to you yet. Give me time." She sat up and scratched his ears. "Finding a girlfriend for a handsome dog like you will be a breeze."

Carrie and Barnaby were still in animated conversation at the dinette table when Dorian returned. He looked up at her with a smile.

"Was everything the way you remembered it?"

"More or less," she answered. "Your property is beautiful."

"You're welcome anytime." He slanted a glance at Carrie. "I hope you'll both be regular visitors."

"I'll be going back to Los Angeles shortly, but I'm sure Carrie would enjoy a respite from the Center now and then," Dorian said artlessly. "Did you have a chance to tell Barnaby about the Center?" she asked Carrie.

"I invited him to stop by and meet some of the members. That's all." Carrie gave Dorian a warning look.

"You think he has something to contribute?" Dorian reminded her obliquely.

"I'm not going to ask him," Carrie answered sharply.

"Will one of you tell me what this is all about?" Barnaby looked at them curiously.

"It's not important," Carrie said before Dorian could reply.

"You never did get around to telling me why you came here today," he mused. "Would this have something to do with it?"

"In a way, but we changed our minds. I never thought it was a good idea, anyway," Carrie said.

"Why don't you let me decide?" Before she could refuse, he said, "I have a suggestion. Let's discuss it over dinner. We can all go into town and give everyone something to talk about for a week."

"I like your spirit." Dorian grinned. "But you two will have to conduct your shock treatment without me. I have an appointment."

Dorian drove back to town alone, feeling a righteous glow of satisfaction. Although Carrie and Barnaby had expressed disappointment that she couldn't join them, they were being courteous rather than sincere. Something was definitely developing there. Carrie might not have gotten her funding, but she wasn't going away empty-handed, either.

Chapter Five

Dorian was bursting to tell Raif about Carrie and Barnaby. He'd be so pleased for his good friend, once he found out how wrong they'd been about "Old Man Richardson."

In spite of her eagerness to share the story, Dorian questioned the advisability of telephoning Raif. She'd made her feelings clear last night; phoning him might send a mixed message. Still, she wouldn't be calling about anything personal, but merely as one friend telling another a piece of news.

Dorian's private debate turned out to be a waste of time. Raif wasn't home. Her disappointment was followed by speculation that brought no joy. Had Raif managed to convince his caller from last night to meet him?

He'd promised to be very convincing, a talent Dorian had reason to remember vividly. Was he using his considerable attractions to persuade some woman at this very moment?

Well, at least it wasn't Linda. She didn't need any coercion. Was it possible Raif wanted to marry her, though, and she liked things the way they were? She might find him more intriguing as a lover than a husband. Raif didn't have any prospects, and Linda had always been materialistic.

If he couldn't see through her, that was *his* problem. Dorian tried to put Raif and his affairs out of her mind, but she couldn't seem to concentrate on anything else. Finally on an impulse, she dialed Linda's number. It was a perfectly valid call. She needed to tell her the house was officially on the market.

After two rings a tape recording was activated: "Hi! This is Linda. I'm not able to come to the phone right now, but your call is very important to me. After the beep, please leave your name, telephone number and any little thing you want to tell me. I'll get back to you soon, I promise."

Listening to Linda's answering machine was almost as annoying as talking to her, Dorian thought disgustedly as she hung up without leaving a message. She must be sensational in bed for any man to put up with her. That wasn't a comforting thought.

Dorian automatically assumed that Raif would show up the next morning. He hadn't said he would, but all those other days he'd simply dropped by without previous arrangement. Dorian kept listening for his truck until midday, when she finally faced the fact that he wasn't coming.

The house was so quiet that she turned on the radio for company as she carefully packed away the knicknacks from her mother's curio cabinet. It was a relief when she ran out of tissue paper. That gave her an excuse to get out of the house for a while.

Dorian found a parking place on Main Street in the shopping section. As she was putting coins in the meter, someone called her name. She looked up to see a tall blond man with a mustache smiling at her.

"I heard you were back in town. It's great to see you again, Dorian."

"How are you, Wayne?" she asked politely. Wayne Shelby had been in her class in high school, but they'd never known each other well.

"I don't suppose you're back to stay."

"No, only for a visit." She didn't feel it necessary to tell him the real reason.

"I run into Sally and Ken every once in a while. They said you're living in L.A. now. How do you like it?"

"It's quite stimulating. What's new with you, Wayne? Are you married?" Dorian felt she ought to show some interest.

"No, I'm still available. So far no one's made me an offer." He laughed.

"You might have to take the initiative," she answered lightly. "What do you do to keep busy?"

"I'm a C.P.A. now," he said proudly. "I have my own office here in Summerville."

"That's wonderful. You were always good in math, as I remember."

He looked pleased. "I didn't think you knew I was alive. Listen, I was just on my way to lunch. Will you join me?"

"I'm sorry, but I have a lot of things to do."

"How about dinner, then?"

Dorian's first impulse was to refuse, but she had second thoughts. Last night she'd sat around all evening wondering what Raif was doing, and tonight promised more of the same. It was time to stop giving Raif such importance. Wayne was pleasant enough, and it might even be fun to talk over old times.

"I'd love to have dinner with you," she said.

Dorian was glad for her decision. There hadn't been any sign of Raif all afternoon, not even a phone call. She faced the fact that there probably wouldn't be one.

Wayne's delight in being with her raised Dorian's spirits. He complimented her appearance, and was touchingly pleased that she'd accepted the date.

"I was crazy about you in high school," he said during dinner at Summerville's best restaurant. "I'll bet you never knew that."

"No, I didn't." She smiled.

"I'm not surprised. Once Raif Dangerfield came on the scene, the rest of us faded into the woodwork."

"That couldn't have bothered you unduly. Weren't you going with Mary Lou Fenway at the time?"

He smiled reminiscently. "I wonder whatever happened to her. After she went east to college, nobody ever heard from her again."

They talked about former classmates, and incidents from their school days. Dorian enjoyed this kind of nostalgia. It didn't touch her emotionally. Raif was hardly mentioned until later in the evening.

They'd gone on to a disco for a nightcap. Dorian was pleasantly relaxed until Wayne began to question her about Raif.

"I suppose you know that Raif is back in town," he remarked casually.

"Yes." Dorian hoped her terse answer would discourage him, but he didn't seem to get the message.

"Is that why you came back to Summerville?"

"Of course not! I didn't even know he was here. We haven't had any contact in years."

"Have you seen him since you're back?"

"We had dinner one night at Sally and Ken's," Dorian answered reluctantly.

"Just like old times, huh?" Wayne asked lightly.

"It's getting late." She reached for her purse. "We'd better go."

He put his hand on her arm. "I'm sorry, Dorian. I didn't mean to pry into your private life."

"Raif isn't part of my life anymore, private or otherwise."

Wayne looked at her with satisfaction. "That's what I wanted to find out."

"Why?" she asked bluntly.

"With Raif out of the picture, maybe there's finally a chance for me."

"That's very flattering, but I live in Los Angeles, remember?"

"It's only a couple of hours away. I get there on business now and then. Could I call you?"

"If you'd like," she answered tepidly.

He was undeterred by her lack of enthusiasm. "Great! I don't want to lose track of you again. I've really enjoyed this evening, Dorian."

"I have, too, Wayne," she answered dutifully.

"Can I see you tomorrow night? Dwight and Francine Johnson are having a party. Will you go with me?"

Dorian hesitated. Raif might be at the party, since he and the Johnsons were close friends. But Sally said Raif seldom saw them. Even if he had accepted an invitation, though, so what? She had no reason to avoid him.

"A lot of the old crowd will be there," Wayne urged. "They'd all like to see you again."

"It sounds delightful," she answered. "What time is the party?"

Raif telephoned Dorian the next day, late in the afternoon. She was caught by surprise, having given up any expectation of hearing from him again. The rush of happiness she felt was beyond her control. She only hoped it didn't show in her voice.

"How's the packing going?" he asked.

"Slowly."

"I'm sorry I deserted you, but I had to go out of town."

"I gathered you were tied up," she answered evenly. "Did you have a nice time?"

"I wouldn't call it a good time, but my trip was very productive." His voice was filled with satisfaction.

Dorian's euphoria dimmed. "I'm very happy for you," she said coldly.

After a slight pause he asked, "Is anything wrong?"

"No, everything is just dandy. This is the best vacation I've ever had."

"Poor baby." His tone was deep and soothing. "You need to get out of the house. How would you feel about a couple of drinks and a nice dinner at the Lotus Grill?"

"It isn't really as good as I remembered," she said sweetly.

"When were you there?"

Dorian was delighted at Raif's surprise. "Last night with Wayne Shelby."

"I see. Well, I guess it was better than staying home alone."

She was furious at his smug assumption that her date had been dull. "I had a wonderful time," she said sharply. "So good, in fact, that I'm going out with Wayne again tonight."

"It sounds like a whirlwind romance," Raif commented.

"I didn't say it was a romance," she replied in annoyance. "I merely said I enjoy his company."

"Evidently, if you're having two intimate dinners in a row with him."

"You're wrong about that, too. We're going to a party at Dwight and Francine Johnson's." She waited to hear if Raif planned to attend also, but he didn't oblige.

"That should be a nice change for you," he remarked pleasantly. "Perhaps it will put you in a better mood."

Dorian's temper flared. Her first impulse was to tell him she was in excellent spirits, but she was too annoyed to sound convincing.

"Thanks for your concern," she said curtly. "It's been nice talking to you, but I have to start getting ready."

"Have a good time," he answered agreeably.

Dorian was determined to follow Raif's suggestion. If he thought she was feeling neglected, he was badly mistaken. When Wayne arrived that evening, the warmth of her greeting surprised and delighted him.

Almost all the people at the party were former acquaintances. Dorian enjoyed seeing them again and finding out what they'd done after high school. In a very short while she didn't have to pretend to be having a good time.

Raif wasn't there, and nobody mentioned him, possibly out of respect for her feelings. Whatever the reason, Dorian was grateful. It was a nice party and she wanted to forget about Raif.

The Johnson house was a fairly new ranch-style with a den almost as large as the living room. The furniture in the den had been pushed back to leave the center of the floor clear for dancing to music from an elaborate stereo system.

Dorian and Wayne were talking to their hostess in the living room when the doorbell rang. Francine left them to answer the door while they continued to chat with the rest of the group. Dorian's back was to the entry, but she realized something was wrong by the expression on the faces of the others. Turning around, she saw the newcomers were Raif and Linda.

Indignation filled Dorian. Raif might have told her he was not only coming to the same party, but bringing Linda as well. He must have known how awkward the situation would be for everyone.

Giving no indication of the anger burning inside her, she said to Wayne, "The music sounds wonderful. Shall we dance?"

As they started toward the den her eyes met Raif's briefly, but she glanced away without speaking. If anyone noticed, that was unfortunate. Dorian didn't trust herself to be civil, not with Linda clinging to his arm with a smug expression on her face.

Dorian wasn't very responsive to Wayne's small talk, but she allowed him to hold her close. He would have been chagrined to know she was hardly aware of him. The evening was spoiled, and she was trying to figure out how soon she could leave without having anyone think it was because of Raif. Or, worse yet, Linda.

Wayne had gone to get them each a drink when Francine approached her. "I'm so sorry, Dorian. I had no idea Raif was coming."

"You mean he crashed the party?" Dorian didn't believe it for a moment.

"Well, not exactly. We invited him, but he said he couldn't make it. I was as surprised as you when he showed up."

"Raif was always unpredictable," Dorian commented grimly.

Francine slanted a troubled glance at her. "I just wanted you to know I would have warned you ahead of time if I'd known."

"It's no big deal." Dorian put a rein on her emotions. "Raif and I are both adults. What happened between us was a long time ago."

"I wasn't sure how you'd feel about seeing him again," Francine said uncertainly.

"We've been in touch since I returned to Summerville."

"That's a load off my mind! I was afraid you might be furious."

"Why? I'm here with someone else, too."

"Oh, but—" Before Francine could complete her sentence, Raif joined them.

"Nice party," he told Francine. "Isn't it, Dorian?"

"The greatest." Dorian smiled brightly, trying to sound as if she meant it.

"I'm so glad you could both come. It's such a happy coincidence. I didn't even know you were in town when I planned the party, Dorian. Of course, I didn't know Raif was coming, either." Francine was babbling out of sheer nervousness. She didn't believe Dorian's assurances for a moment.

"We're full of surprises," Raif said smoothly.

"You are, anyway," Dorian said.

"If you'll excuse me, I have to... uh... I have to speak to Dwight." Francine left them abruptly.

"Why didn't you tell me you planned to be here?" Dorian demanded when she and Raif were alone.

"I didn't think you were interested in my activities."

"I am when you do something this thoughtless."

"What have I done?" He managed to sound puzzled.

"It's no secret that Linda and I detested each other in high school. Everyone is waiting to find out how I'll react to seeing you together."

"We've been divorced for a long time," Raif replied casually. "Why should anybody be surprised that we're dating other people?"

"They wouldn't be, if it was anyone except Linda."

"I think you're overreacting, but if it makes you feel any better, Linda isn't my date tonight."

"You just happened to meet at the front door?" Dorian asked scornfully.

"No, I brought her, but only as a favor. Her date got tied up at the office and couldn't make it until later. She didn't want to wait around for him, so she called to ask for a ride."

Dorian stared at him uncertainly. "Are you telling me the truth?"

His face was impassive as he gazed back at her. "Why would I lie about something so trivial?"

Her lashes fell. "Maybe I *was* overreacting. I'm sorry."

"I forgive you." He slid his arm around her waist and drew her close. When she gave him a startled look, Raif smiled. "Now that we've made up, let's dance."

They joined the other couples on the floor, their bodies conforming perfectly. Part of Dorian's mind registered pleasure, but her thoughts were busy with something else. Raif didn't seem upset that Linda had a date with another man. If she wasn't the woman on the phone that night, who was?

"You're very quiet," Raif remarked. "Are you still upset with me?"

"No, I was just wondering about something."

"Involving me?"

Dorian was sorry she'd brought it up. "It isn't important."

Raif noticed Wayne in the doorway carrying a couple of glasses. As he started the scan the room, Raif guided Dorian to the French doors leading to the backyard.

"This is better," he said smoothly. Taking her hand he led her to the end of the garden. "It's too noisy in there to talk."

"Wayne is probably looking for me" she said doubtfully.

"I'll take you back in a few minutes. First I want to know what's bothering you."

She could have lied or made up something trivial, but Dorian felt a compulsion to know who the other woman was. It was like probing a sore spot, even though you knew it was going to hurt.

"I jumped to conclusions about you and Linda," she began carefully.

"I hope you're finally convinced that you're wrong."

"Yes."

He looked at her closely. "But now something else is troubling you."

"I'm not troubled, just curious," she said defensively.

"About what?"

"It's none of my business, but we *were* married to each other, so it's natural for me to be interested in your welfare." The words came out in a rush.

"Wouldn't it be easier if you just came out and asked me what you want to know?" he asked patiently.

"I wondered who the woman was who telephoned you."

"What woman? When?" He stared at her blankly.

"The night I had dinner at your house."

His expression was unreadable. "What makes you think it was a woman?"

"I couldn't help overhearing your conversation," Dorian answered uncomfortably. "And afterward you said how important the call was to you. I could tell, anyway. You were all wound up."

"Is that why you left so abruptly?"

"No! Certainly not." She had to preserve her pride. "I'm delighted if you've found someone to care about. The only reason I brought it up was out of concern. I'd like to think she's someone who's right for you."

"Unlike Linda?" he teased.

"I certainly hope so! I want you to be happy, Raif."

"That's very sweet," he answered huskily.

"Do I know her?" Dorian persisted.

"There isn't any other woman, honey. The call you overheard was from a man I've been trying to persuade to help me. If I seemed tense, it was because he was giving me excuses."

The constricting band around Dorian's heart loosened, and she suddenly realized what she'd been denying all along. She was still in love with Raif! The knowledge that she hadn't lost him to another woman made her almost giddy with joy.

"I would have told you all about it if you'd stayed longer," he said.

"Is that what you were going to tell me? I thought—"

"What did you think?" he prodded gently when she didn't continue.

"That you'd met someone who was important to you," she murmured.

Tiny pinpoints of light sparkled in his eyes as he cupped her chin in his palm and forced her to look at him. "Would you have minded?"

As they gazed into each other's eyes, footsteps sounded on the gravel path. Raif's hand dropped to his side, and Dorian turned away to compose herself. Just the touch of his long fingers made her heart race.

Wayne appeared, looking annoyed. "So this is where you are! I've been hunting everywhere for you."

"I'm sorry, Wayne." Dorian really wasn't, but she realized he had a legitimate complaint. "It was so noisy in there that we came outside for a few minutes."

"More like half an hour," he said tightly.

"It didn't seem that long," Raif remarked innocently.

As Wayne gave him an outraged look, Dorian said hurriedly, "We had a lot to talk about. Raif has been out of town, and I didn't have a chance until now to tell him about Old Man Richardson."

Raif's amused expression changed to interest. "The recluse who used to chase us off his property? What about him?"

"You wouldn't believe how wrong we were." Dorian turned to Wayne, trying to include him in the conversation. "You remember Mr. Richardson. He's the one who bought the old Hempstead estate on the outskirts of town. We used to swim in his pond when we were teenagers."

"I know the place you're talking about, but I was never there," Wayne said.

"What about Richardson?" Raif prompted.

Dorian gave him an abridged version of her visit with Carrie. "He couldn't have been nicer to us—especially Carrie." Dorian laughed. "I wouldn't be a bit surprised if a romance developed there."

"Who is Carrie?" Wayne asked, looking increasingly frustrated.

"Carrie Madison, a woman who's very active in the Senior Citizen's Center," Dorian explained.

"I don't know her, either," Wayne said.

"Wouldn't it be terrific if they got together?" Raif asked Dorian. "They're the right age for each other."

"But more than that, they're both such vital people. They could have a really full life together."

Dorian and Raif were so caught up in her news that they unwittingly ignored Wayne. At least, Dorian's neglect was unintentional.

After a few minutes he gave up trying to get her attention. "I'll be inside, in case you care," he told her glumly.

"Wait, Wayne! I'll go with you." She felt guilty about her treatment of him. Poor Wayne. She wasn't being a very satisfactory date. With a rueful smile at Raif, Dorian went back into the house.

Raif didn't stay long at the party. After he left, Dorian lost interest, too, although she tried to conceal the fact.

Wayne wasn't fooled by her bright smiles and superficial chatter. When they were saying good-night at her front door he said, "I'm sorry tonight didn't work out."

"I had a lovely time," she protested.

"But not because of me. It isn't over between you and Raif, is it?"

"I apologized for going outside without telling you," she answered evasively.

"You know that's not what I mean."

Dorian didn't want to admit anything at this point. Not until she found out how Raif felt. "I suppose you always feel something for a person you've been married to," she said carefully.

"I thought divorce was supposed to take care of that. I guess I should have known I didn't stand a chance."

"I've really enjoyed getting to know you better, Wayne." She didn't know what else to say.

"I'd hoped to get to know you a *lot* better." He smiled a little sadly. "At least I got farther than I did in high school. In another eight years I might get up enough nerve to kiss you."

"Don't waste those years on me, Wayne. You have too much to offer some lucky woman."

He took both of her hands. "I hope Raif knows how fortunate he is."

Dorian didn't wait for Raif to telephone her the next morning. She called him. "Are you coming over today?" she asked without beating around the bush.

"Do you want me to?"

"Yes."

"It's such a beautiful day out. Much too nice to stay indoors and clean closets, or whatever you had planned."

Her heart plunged. Raif hadn't counted the hours till he could see *her*, obviously. "You're one of the grasshoppers of the world," she answered lightly to hide her disappointment. "I'm one of the ants."

"Even an ant takes the day off on a national holiday."

"What holiday is today?"

"Independence Day."

"That's the Fourth of July," she objected.

"This is the other independence day. The one where you say, I'm fed up and I need some relaxation. How about it? Can I persuade you to do something purely frivolous with me?"

Dorian's heart soared back to its accustomed place. "What did you have in mind?"

"Whatever you like. As long as it isn't educational, or classified as work."

"That rules out the public library and driving anywhere on the freeway."

"Those wouldn't be my first choices. What would you really like to do?"

Anything with you, was Dorian's silent response. Aloud, she said, "You choose. Ants don't have much experience at goofing off."

"It gets easier with practice. You start by using respectable names like stress relief, or quality time management."

"Okay, manage my time qualitatively."

"Now you're getting the hang of it," he said approvingly. "Well, let's see. It's a gorgeous day, so we want to do something outdoors. I know! Let's take a picnic lunch up to the old pond. Ever since you told me about Richardson last night, I've been itching to get a look at him."

"I don't think that's such a good idea," Dorian said doubtfully.

"You said he was Mr. Hospitality."

"He was, but I didn't have a chance to tell you the whole story." She related the tragic circumstances of Barnaby's wife and daughter. "We'd have to ask his permission, and I'm afraid the pond has bad vibes for him."

"If he wants to stop living in a vacuum, he has to confront the past."

"That's true, but I'd feel funny about asking him."

"You'd be doing him a favor," Raif urged.

"I don't know. Maybe I'd better check with Carrie first and find out how their dinner in town went."

"Phone her, and call me back."

Dorian spent the next hour on the telephone. She was a little diffident about asking if the evening was a success. Their friendship wasn't that close yet. But Dorian's misgivings were unnecessary. Carrie was eager to talk about Barnaby.

"He's been all over the world, and he's so well informed on everything that's going on," she confided. "It's amazing how much information a person can get in his own home."

"Well, that's what I wanted to ask you about," Dorian said tentatively.

"Not that Barnaby is really isolated," Carrie rushed on. "Do you know he plays chess by mail with a man in Australia? He also keeps in touch with friends all over the country."

"That's nice, but how does he relate to people here in Summerville?" Dorian asked bluntly. "Did he panic when you went to a restaurant?"

"Of course not!" Carrie was indignant. "You're implying the poor man is some kind of freak. We had a perfectly delightful dinner at the Lotus Grill."

"Did you see anyone you knew?"

"As a matter of fact, I did. Martha and Denny Ratigan were there. I introduced Barnaby to them. Why are you asking me these strange questions?"

Dorian explained about Raif's plans for the day. "I thought I'd better check with you first to see if you think Barnaby really welcomes visitors."

"You'll have to ask him, but I'm sure he does. He was quite cordial to the Ratigans. Do you know what he said to me several times?"

Dorian was treated to an in-depth account of Carrie's evening with Barnaby. Her hunch about them was correct. They were very compatible. Dorian was happy for the other woman, but Carrie showed no signs of running down.

When she could get a word in, Dorian said, "I'd love to hear more, but Raif is waiting for me to call back."

First she had to phone Barnaby, who was very receptive. "By all means come and enjoy yourselves. I meant it when I said you were welcome anytime."

"That's very nice of you. We're bringing a picnic lunch, but I promise to cart everything away when we leave."

"I'm not worried about that, but why don't you let me prepare lunch here instead?"

"Oh no, I wouldn't hear of it."

"It's no trouble, I assure you. In fact, I just had another idea," Barnaby said in a casual voice. "Why don't you bring Carrie along, too?"

Dorian gave every polite excuse she could think of. The truth was, she wanted to be alone with Raif. But in his courteous way, Barnaby wouldn't take no for an answer.

Finally Dorian gave in. She had one last hope. "I'll have to call Carrie. She might not be free at the last minute like this."

First Dorian phoned Raif to tell him about the new development. His reaction didn't delight her.

"That's great! They really seem to have hit it off," he said. "You must be very proud of yourself."

"That isn't the word I'd use," she answered ironically.

"Don't be modest, honey," he said fondly. "You've always been a good friend."

"What do you want for lunch?" she asked abruptly. "I still think we should bring our own."

Carrie had accepted the invitation with enthusiasm, and the logistics were decided on. They needed to take Raif's truck, since Dorian's sports car was a two-seater.

Dorian hard-boiled eggs and made sandwiches without enthusiasm. The afternoon would probably be more fun than cleaning out drawers, but this wasn't the day she'd envisioned. Maybe she'd just been kidding herself, though. If Raif only wanted to be friends, it was better this way.

In spite of Dorian's objections, Barnaby had prepared lunch for them. "I have a picnic hamper full of sandwiches," she protested.

"I'm sure you young people will get hungry during the afternoon," he said.

Raif grinned. "I like you, Barnaby. It's been years since I thought of myself as a young person."

Barnaby returned his smile. "Stewardesses don't call you sir, do they? That's when you know you're over the hill."

"Or when policemen remind you of your nephews," Carrie added.

They all got along together as though they'd known each other for years. Lunch was a relaxed affair in spite of the formal surroundings. Barnaby had set the table in the dining room with beautiful china and sterling silver flatware.

"You shouldn't have gone to all this trouble," Carrie protested.

His eyes twinkled. "This is to distract you from the food."

It became obvious that he was joking when they tasted the three-course lunch Barnaby had prepared. A cold gazpacho soup was followed by green-chile quiche, accompanied by a platter of fresh fruit. Dessert was rocky road ice cream and cookies.

Carrie exclaimed over every course. "I can't believe you made all of this."

"Well, I did have a little help from the freezer section at Petroni's." He mentioned an upscale market in Larkin. "But I made the soup."

"It was delicious," Carrie declared. "I'm really impressed."

"Men aren't as helpless in the kitchen as they pretend to be," Dorian said. "Raif is a great cook, too, and I never knew it."

"I didn't develop my skills until after our divorce," Raif told the others.

"I didn't know you—" Barnaby cut off his surprised remark with a look of discomfort.

"Don't be embarrassed," Raif told him. "It's common knowledge, and Dorian and I are the best of friends."

"Amicable divorces are very prevalent these days," Carrie remarked brightly.

Dorian's chest felt tight as she remembered the bitterness of their breakup. She changed the subject abruptly. "Where is Toby? I haven't seen him around today. Toby is Barnaby's dog," she explained to Raif.

"He's a very intimidating animal," Carrie said.

"What kind of dog is he?" Raif asked.

"A giant schnauzer," Barnaby replied. "He's really very friendly, but people are put off by his size."

"Your first thought on meeting Toby is to hope he's a vegetarian," Dorian said.

"I'd like to see him," Raif remarked.

"He's probably roaming around in the woods. He'll show up sooner or later," Barnaby said.

"Your grounds are magnificent. You have the best of both worlds out here," Dorian commented. "You're close to town, yet you have the peacefulness of the country."

"Untouched acres like these are getting scarce," Carrie observed. "Even Summerville is being blighted by mini-malls. Why can't developers leave well enough alone? They're destroying our small-town character."

"I'm not beating the drum for malls, but they do provide jobs and generate income, which Summerville badly needs," Raif said.

"According to friends of ours, the economy here isn't in great shape," Dorian said.

"While I sympathize with Carrie's desire to keep Summerville the way it is, the town needs to attract small industry," Barnaby said. "I can't understand why it hasn't. Living is certainly easier here than in the big cities."

"Adequate housing," Raif answered succinctly. "Businesses aren't going to relocate to a place where their employees can't find a place to live."

"My house is on the market, and I haven't been besieged by offers," Dorian objected.

"I'm talking about *affordable* housing. Your home is too big and too expensive for a young couple. This area needs a development of small houses with low-interest financing."

Barnaby was regarding him speculatively. "You sound as if you've given this a lot of thought."

"I grew up in Summerville," Raif answered. "I don't want to see it wither away. Too many people are leaving because they can't find work."

"Is there enough land to build on?"

"Not right in town, but certainly on the outskirts. You might not be happy about it, but I'm considering—" Raif broke off with a swift glance at Dorian. "It seems to me the acreage adjoining your property would be ideal."

"Why would I mind?" Barnaby asked.

"Your privacy should remain intact, but you *would* have neighbors for the first time."

"I've already gotten the feeling that my life is going to change." Barnaby smiled as his eyes rested on Carrie.

Her cheeks turned a becoming pink, and she reached for the silver coffeepot. "Can I pour anyone more coffee?"

When they all declined, their host said to Raif and Dorian, "I'm sure you want to take advantage of the sun. Don't let us keep you."

"I'll help with the dishes first," Dorian said.

"I wouldn't think of it," Barnaby answered. "You're a guest."

"I'll help Barnaby clear up." Carrie was firm when he started to protest. "You two run along."

"Will you join us later?" Dorian asked politely.

"We'll see," Carrie replied vaguely.

When they were outside, Dorian asked Raif, "Did you get the feeling they were happy to get rid of us?"

"Don't take it personally." He chuckled. "Remember when we first met? We wanted to be alone, too."

I still do, Dorian thought somberly. Too bad Raif didn't share that desire.

Chapter Six

By the time Dorian and Raif reached the pond she felt more cheerful. The lovely sylvan spot brought back memories of a happier time.

"See, nothing has changed," she told him. When Raif didn't answer immediately she turned and surprised an unreadable expression on his face.

"You can count on nature, if nothing else," he said, but his voice was light. "We'll soon find out if the water is as cold as ever."

"Shouldn't we wait a while after that big lunch?" she asked as he began to unbutton his shirt.

"The water is only five feet deep. You'd have to kneel down to drown. But we can wait for half an hour if you'd rather."

"It might be a good idea," she answered absently.

Dorian was watching Raif undress. After shrugging off his shirt, he unzipped his jeans and pushed them down his

narrow hips and muscular legs. The brief bathing trunk
he wore under the jeans looked even whiter against his
deep tan.

Dorian searched for some imperfection, some sign of
aging, but Raif's body was superb. In another age he
would have been a Roman gladiator or a Greek athlete,
anything that required strength and suppleness.

He glanced over with raised eyebrows. ''Aren't you going to take off your clothes?''

Her cheeks felt suddenly hot. She'd almost blurted out
the words that sprang to her lips. *You used to do that for
me.*

Raif was puzzled by her silence. ''Don't you have your
suit on underneath?''

''Yes, of course! I . . . I was daydreaming.''

''This place is certainly full of memories.'' He rested his
hands on his hips and stared out at the leafy trees ringing
the pond. ''I can hardly believe how young and naive we
were in those days.''

''Don't the two go together?''

''I suppose so.''

Raif turned around and started to watch Dorian dis-
robe, as she'd watched him. She would have been gratified by the brilliant light in his eyes, but when she glanced
up it disappeared. He took a blanket out of their beach bag
and spread it on the ground under a tree.

''We won't get any sun there,'' Dorian objected.

''You can't take much sun.'' He looked at her objec-
tively. ''Your midsection is as white as milk.''

She was annoyed and frustrated. Was that all Raif saw
when he looked at her? She was wearing a bikini that most
men would have found sexy, and she thought her figure
was actually better than when she had been a teenager.

Raif could barely keep his desire under control in those days. Now, she might as well have been his sister.

"You must not get outdoors much," he commented.

"That's the price of working for a living," she replied tersely.

"Too bad."

She looked at him sharply, but his expression was bland. Raif had stretched out on the blanket with a contented sigh.

"Ahh, this is the life. A perfect day, an idyllic setting and a beautiful girl."

"Thanks for the bottom billing," she said dryly.

"I called you beautiful," he pointed out.

"I didn't think you noticed."

"It would be difficult not to in a suit like that."

"Bikinis are considered tame nowadays," she said, lying down next to him. "That bathing suit they call the thong is all the rage."

"So I've heard."

Raif sounded disinterested, but Dorian persisted. "In Europe they're even more uninhibited. A lot of women go topless and no one thinks anything of it." When he didn't respond, she said, "I wonder what it would feel like."

A muscle twitched at the point of his firm jaw, but his voice was even. "Be my guest."

"I didn't mean now," she answered hastily. "I was just trying to imagine how it would feel to be half-naked in public."

"No, you wanted *me* to imagine you that way." Anger flared in his eyes as he sat up and stared down at her. "You never used to be a tease, Dorian."

"I didn't—I wasn't trying—" She stumbled to a halt.

"You could have fooled me." His face was hard. "Shall I demonstrate what happens to women who play games?"

"No!" Dorian had never seen Raif like this. Naked lust glittered in his eyes.

She started to scramble to her feet, but he was too quick for her. His body covered hers, forcing her onto her back. Both arms were pinned under her, so she couldn't push him away.

"Let go of me this—"

His mouth cut off her words. Dorian tried to twist her head away, but he held her chin in a viselike grip. While his tongue plundered her mouth, he began an intimate exploration of her body.

She writhed without success as he stroked her breast and rotated his thumb over the vulnerable tip. When his fingers slipped inside her bikini bra, an inadvertent moan was wrenched from her throat. Her treacherous body was reacting to him, even while her brain heatedly denounced his actions.

This was an assault, not an act of love. Raif was punishing her unjustly. She'd only wanted to recapture some of the old magic, to find out if any remained for him. When her wild rejection didn't deter him, Dorian's body finally relaxed in exhaustion. She was no match for Raif. The weight of his hard frame made her feel like a pressed flower.

When she stopped struggling, he shifted his weight so her arms were released. Although she could have gotten away, Dorian remained motionless with her eyes closed. She didn't want him to see the tears that were dampening her lashes.

"Whether you believe it or not, that was for your own good," he said softly.

"Am I supposed to say thank you?" Bitterness filled her voice.

He smoothed the tumbled hair off her forehead. "You're an amazingly beautiful woman. If you send signals like that to the wrong man, he won't stop the way I did."

"I believe you've made your point. Now, would you please leave me alone?"

"That's hard to—" His fingertips had trailed across her cheek to her closed eyelids. "Are you crying?"

"You hurt me," she said indignantly, although he hadn't.

Raif had restrained her with a minimum of force. His kiss had held anger, but it didn't qualify as brutal. Dorian was devastated because all she'd provoked in him was fury and lust.

He framed her face in both hands and kissed her gently. "I never meant to hurt you."

As they gazed into each other's eyes, a sweet tide of longing swept over her. All the hurt was blotted out by Raif's face, just inches from hers. His green eyes had darkened to the color of jade, and she could feel the whisper of his breath on her parted lips.

Her heart was beating rapidly, reacting to the charged atmosphere between them. The sudden tension in his muscles showed he felt it, too. Suddenly a loud crackling came from the bushes lining the path to the house.

Raif's expression changed as he sat up. Dorian recovered more slowly, wondering how she could make polite conversation with anyone when her entire body was still vibrating.

The bushes parted and Toby trotted into the clearing. He stopped when he caught sight of them, then raced over as he recognized Dorian.

"What a great dog," Raif exclaimed in surprise. He scratched Toby's ears.

Dorian struggled to match Raif's composure. "That's the right adjective for him, all right."

"I wonder if he swims."

"A dog that size can do anything he pleases."

"Let's find out." Raif picked up a pinecone and showed it to the dog before skipping it into the pond. "Okay, fella, fetch."

Toby watched the widening ripples, then looked back at Raif without expression.

"Does that satisfy your curiosity?" Dorian asked.

"The test wasn't conclusive. He might know how to swim, but he just doesn't feel like it at the moment."

"You've overlooked a third possibility. That he's too smart to expend all that energy on a pinecone."

"It's the best I could do. We left the sandwiches up at the house."

Dorian smiled. "You know how young people are. We'd forget our heads if they weren't attached to our necks."

Raif grinned back at her. "Let's go swimming before Barnaby and Carrie show up and tell us it's too soon to go in the water."

Any residual tension vanished as they splashed around lightheartedly while Toby sat on the grass like a sentinel. Finally Dorian turned on her back and floated with outstretched arms, admiring the dappled sunshine that filtered through the trees.

Raif swam over and stood beside her. His broad shoulders were above the water line, tan and glistening. Dorian wanted to reach out and draw a line between the little droplets that freckled his smooth skin, but she was too diffident.

He felt no such constraint. Sketching a pattern on her stomach he said, "Better be careful or you'll get sunburned in a leaf design. That would be a little bizarre."

"Nobody would see it but me," she answered without thinking.

His hand stilled. "What are you telling me, Dorian?"

She pushed his hand away, chagrined at herself. The last thing she wanted was for Raif to know there was no other man in her life.

"We'd better get back to the others before they come looking for us," she said, wading toward the bank.

He followed and watched without comment as she toweled her hair and then dried her arms and legs. Although she didn't glance at him, Dorian was achingly conscious of Raif's sculptured body.

"Our trip into the past wasn't a howling success, was it?" he asked quietly.

"I didn't expect anything different," she lied.

After a moment's silence he asked, "Are we still friends?"

"Is that what you'd call us? We seem to go from one pitched battle to another."

"Why do you think that is?" he asked softly.

"Possibly because we don't have anything in common anymore. Our lives have taken different directions."

"Would you feel more kindly toward me if I were a success?" He watched her intently.

That had nothing to do with her feelings. It was disappointing to see him give up—she wanted him to fulfill all his hopes and dreams—but it didn't alter her love. Raif didn't want her love, however, merely her good opinion.

Dorian chose her words carefully. "You always had such ambitious plans for the future. I'm a little surprised that you've lowered your sights, but it's your life."

He smiled mirthlessly. "Aren't you lucky you don't have to share it."

"That's unworthy of you," she answered stiffly. "I didn't marry you for your prospects, nor would I have walked out on you if they'd failed to materialize."

"I'm sorry. That remark *was* uncalled for. I guess I'm a little disappointed, too." He folded the blanket and picked up the beach bag. "Let's go collect Carrie."

The other couple was sitting on the terrace with tall drinks in their hands. Barnaby raised his glass. "We started without you. What would you like to drink?"

"Nothing for me, thanks," Dorian declined. "It's a little too early in the day."

"It's almost five o'clock," Carrie said.

"It can't be that late already," Dorian exclaimed.

"Time flies when you're having fun." Only Dorian noticed that Raif's smile was sardonic.

"You must have enjoyed your swim," Carrie commented. "We expected you back sooner."

"I'll bet you spent the afternoon watching the clock," Raif teased.

"We managed to keep each other amused." Barnaby chuckled. "At least I hope Carrie wasn't too bored."

"You know better." She smiled at him before turning to the others. "Barnaby just returned from a trip to New York to visit friends and see some shows. He says that big Broadway musical is everything it's touted to be."

Raif raised one eyebrow. "You're somewhat of a fraud, Barnaby."

The older man looked at him in surprise. "Why do you say that?"

"All this time the town has been thinking of you as an eccentric recluse, while in reality you've been leading a full life."

Barnaby flicked a glance at Carrie. "Not as full as it might have been."

Raif's mouth curved wryly. "We all have regrets about one thing or another."

"I didn't realize the reputation I'd acquired. I was shocked when Carrie and Dorian were afraid of me."

"The shock was mutual," Dorian remarked. "People don't normally carry axes while greeting visitors."

"I'll bet it discourages door-to-door salesmen," Raif said, grinning.

"You never did get around to telling me what brought you here," Barnaby said to Carrie.

"It was just a notion of Dorian's," she answered dismissively.

"Are you a reporter for one of those tabloid newspapers?" He looked at Dorian curiously. "Were you expecting to get a lurid story?"

"Nothing like that." In spite of Carrie's urgent, though silent warning, Dorian told him why they'd visited him that day.

"It sounds like a worthwhile project. I'd be happy to underwrite it," he said when she'd finished.

"That's very generous of you," Dorian said. "You don't have to pick up the whole tab, though. A donation will be appreciated."

Barnaby shrugged. "There isn't that much money involved. Why didn't you want to tell me about this?" he asked Carrie.

She looked troubled. "I was afraid a program involving children would bring back unhappy memories."

"You're a very nice lady, but your worries are misplaced." His voice was gentle. "I can't think of a better tribute to my daughter."

"You're quite a guy, Barnaby," Raif said.

"I've made my peace with life," he answered simply. "The loss of a child is devastating. You become angry and bitter, and you want to blame someone. Ultimately you realize that's self-destructive. Nothing can change the past, but you can't let it warp your entire future. It took a long time before I was able to pick up the pieces and start over.''

"That's certainly understandable,'' Carrie said sympathetically.

Dorian sat very still as the conversation continued around her. Barnaby's quiet words had struck a nerve. Had she been guilty of the same irrational behavior—with a lot less excuse? Raif had been there to comfort her, but she'd rejected him. No wonder he'd thought she was too young to have married. For the first time, she wondered if he could have been right.

"Then it's all settled. Is tomorrow night okay with you, Dorian?'' Raif was looking at her questioningly.

"For what?'' she asked blankly.

"We just had a long discussion about dinner at my house. Weren't you listening?''

"I'm afraid I was thinking about something else,'' she confessed.

"Are you free tomorrow night?''

"I think I can fit you into my busy social schedule.'' She smiled.

"Summerville must seem very boring to you after Los Angeles,'' Carrie observed.

"Not really. It's a pleasant change. Normally I'd be putting in long hours at the office.''

"That means you enjoy your work,'' Barnaby said.

"I do. I've been accused of being married to it,'' she answered ruefully.

"A pretty girl like you? I find that hard to believe,'' he protested. "Succeeding in business is rewarding, but you should also take time to enjoy yourself.''

"People enjoy themselves in different ways," Raif said impassively.

Every time her success was mentioned, Raif became withdrawn, Dorian thought hopelessly. How could she convince him that they weren't in competition? All she wanted was his approval.

Sensing an undercurrent, Barnaby dropped the subject. "Can I freshen anyone's drink?"

"Not mine, thanks," Dorian declined.

"We'd better be starting home. Are you ready, Carrie?" Raif asked.

On the way home they discussed Barnaby's generous offer. "Do you think I should accept?" Carrie asked.

Raif shrugged. "Why not? He's loaded."

"I don't want to take advantage of him," Carrie said doubtfully. "He might have felt obligated."

"Barnaby had no ties to Summerville," Raif pointed out.

"That's just it. He doesn't have any reason to feel kindly toward the town. Nobody ever went out of their way for him."

"They will now. This is a great opportunity to ease him back into the mainstream."

"Barnaby doesn't have to buy approval," Carrie said indignantly.

"Nobody should have to, and I don't think that's his intent. He seems genuinely interested."

"It *would* give people a chance to see what a fine person he is."

"*You* certainly made up your mind about him in a hurry," Raif teased.

"Women use their intuition about these things," she answered demurely.

"You happen to be right about Barnaby, but I wouldn't put too much faith in intuition. Charm can cover a multitude of sins."

"You're too cynical. A person shouldn't automatically suspect the worst of someone. Isn't that right, Dorian?" Carrie asked, to enlist another woman's support.

When Dorian hesitated, Raif asked mockingly, "Aren't you going to answer the question?"

Dorian stared straight ahead, but she could feel his eyes on her flushed face. Would the past dog her forever? She chose her words carefully. "Sometimes it's difficult not to pass judgment. A lot of things can influence people."

"Would you agree that some of those things are emotional?" Raif demanded.

Carrie darted a nervous look at them. "My goodness, I didn't mean to provoke a serious discussion."

Raif smiled without humor. "You happened to hit on a basic difference of opinion between Dorian and me. We won't ever agree, but we've managed to strike an uneasy truce."

"That's nice," Carrie said vaguely, then added hastily, "About tomorrow night...what can I bring?"

"Not a thing. I can handle it."

"I'm sure you can. You're very capable, but it was so nice of you to invite us. I'd like to help."

"Be careful, I might stick you with the cleaning up." He grinned.

"Don't let him scare you. He has a dishwasher." Dorian joined the conversation to take her mind off Raif's proximity.

She was sitting in the middle, which meant her left shoulder, hip and thigh came in contact with Raif's, no matter how hard she tried to avoid it. The enforced intimacy didn't seem to bother him one bit. His rangy body was completely relaxed in the driver's seat. She could have been a sack of potatoes propped up next to him for all the interest he took.

"I hope your dishwasher does a better job than the one we have at the Center," Carrie said to Raif. "If I don't rinse the glasses really well before I put them in, they don't come out clean."

"Maybe your water isn't hot enough," he said.

"Would that make a difference?"

"Definitely. A lot of service calls are unnecessary. All a repair man has to do is turn up the temperature."

"Well, it's certainly worth a try. How do I go about it?"

"I'll do it for you after we drop Dorian off."

"I don't know how I'd manage without you, Raif," Carrie said fondly.

"Glad to be of help." As he pulled up in front of Dorian's house Raif leaned out the window and waved at Sally, who was watering her front lawn. "Hi, Sally, what's doing?"

"Wait a minute, I'll be right over." She turned off the hose and came across the street to the truck. After Raif had introduced her to Carrie, Sally announced, "A real estate man brought someone to look at your house today, Dorrie."

"That's an event," Dorian said.

"Could be. They stayed a long time, and then they stood around outside talking."

"Sounds as if they're interested. You might be lucky enough to make a quick sale," Raif told Dorian.

She was stung by his casual tone of voice. It obviously didn't matter to him that they wouldn't see each other anymore. "Wouldn't that be wonderful?" she exclaimed, to show him she didn't care, either.

Sally's face was doleful. "I'm trying to be happy for you, but it won't be the same, having strangers living in your house."

"It's better than letting it stand empty. I wouldn't be here either way."

Sally smiled wryly. "Why am I complaining? I don't see that much of you when you're here."

"Not enough," Dorian agreed.

"We can remedy that tomorrow night," Raif said. "How would you and Ken like to have dinner at my house? Dorian and Carrie are coming."

"I never turn down a meal I don't have to cook," Sally said promptly. "What time would you like us to be there?"

"Seven o'clock will be fine." Raif turned to Dorian. "Can I pick you up a half hour earlier so I can do a couple of last-minute things?"

"We can bring Dorrie," Sally offered. "Why should you have to go out when we live right across the street?"

"That would make it easier. Would you mind?" he asked Dorian.

"Why should I mind?"

Raif didn't seem to notice the shadows that darkened her blue eyes. "Okay, then we're all set. Now I'll see what I can do about Carrie's dishwasher."

After they'd driven away, Sally said, "Tomorrow night sounds like fun. Is Raif having a big party?"

"Just six of us as far as I know. Raif is very unpredictable."

Dorian's suppressed emotion was visible to Sally, at least. "You don't mind that Raif invited Kenny and me?" she asked uncertainly.

"Of course not! What gave you that idea?"

"Well, you might have had things to talk to Raif about. If it was only going to be the two of you I might have checked with you before accepting, but he said Carrie was coming."

"She is, but you'd be welcome anyway. Raif and I don't have a date. This is just an impromptu get-together, like the one at your house."

Dorian's brittle tone indicated there was more to the story, but her set expression didn't invite questions. Sally prudently changed the subject. "Carrie is an attractive woman, isn't she? Is her husband nice?"

"She's a widow."

"You said there'd be six of us."

"There will be. You'll never guess who else is coming."

After Dorian told Sally about Barnaby, they discussed him at length. Sally had to hear all the details. By the time Dorian finally went into the house, she was feeling more cheerful.

The mood faded when she started to think about Raif again. He was never out of her thoughts for long lately, which was an omen of disaster. Raif's actions showed how little she meant to him. A man who had any interest in her wouldn't have accepted Sally's offer to drive her to his house. Which naturally meant they'd take her home. It was fairly evident that Raif didn't want to be alone with her.

How ironic that their roles were reversed. He was rejecting *her* now. Would it help if she told him she was sorry about everything? No, Dorian concluded mournfully. He was sorry, too. They hadn't meant to hurt each other. It had simply worked out that way, and there was nothing she could do about it except try to remain friends.

After Raif had performed the simple task of adjusting Carrie's thermostat, she offered him coffee. "Unless you're in a hurry to get home."

He gave her a twisted smile. "Coffee would be nice. Nobody's waiting to read me the riot act if I'm late."

"That's one of the joys of living alone," Carrie remarked casually. "You can come home when you want, go to bed when you want, do whatever you like. Nobody cares."

Raif concentrated on stirring his coffee. "That's right. Nobody cares."

"Of course men enjoy being single more than women do."

"You think so?"

"It stands to reason. Look at the opportunities they have."

"If you're talking about sex, that's kid stuff. A real man doesn't have to keep proving his masculinity."

"Then why do you suppose so many men choose to remain single?" Carrie asked innocently. "Take you, for example. You'd make a terrific husband."

"I obviously wasn't," he answered curtly.

"It's foolish to let one mistake sour you on the whole institution. You and Dorian should both remarry."

"She probably will." Raif's profile looked carved from stone.

"I certainly hope so. It would be sad if she spent her life alone."

"What about the joys of doing what you please? Didn't you just tell me how great it is?"

"I lied." She smiled mischievously. "It's plain hell to come home to an empty house."

"According to Dorian, she isn't home much. She's completely wrapped up in her work."

Carrie tried to mask her irritation. "Has it ever occurred to you that she might be exaggerating a trifle?"

"I'm sure she's as successful as she says, and I couldn't be prouder of her." His face softened. "She was an enchanting young girl, and she's blossomed into a beautiful, talented woman."

"I think she appreciates *your* qualities, too," Carrie remarked dryly.

The light went out of Raif's eyes. "Our divorce was traumatic, but we've managed to become friends."

"Are you this blind about all women, or only Dorian?" Carrie demanded. "Anyone can see you're both still attracted to each other."

"There was always a strong sexual attraction between us. What's your point?"

"I think it's more than that."

"Your woman's intuition again?" he asked mockingly.

"Not entirely. I've seen the way she looks at you, and how hurt she is by your indifference."

"You don't know what you're talking about," Raif said roughly. "I'd never hurt Dorian."

"Not deliberately, but that's what you're doing. I have no right to meddle in your lives, but I'm so fond of both of you. I hate to see you mess up your second chance at happiness because of crossed signals."

Raif pushed his chair back abruptly and walked over to the window. He stared out at the straggly grass with his fists jammed in his pockets.

"I know you mean well, Carrie, but you don't understand the problem. Dorian thinks I let her down when she needed me, and maybe I did. Sometimes it's better to tell the person you love what she wants to hear. I told the truth and destroyed her faith in me."

"But you were youngsters then. That was a long time ago."

"Faith doesn't renew itself," he answered grimly.

"That's nonsense! Dorian isn't a vindictive person."

"I know that. She might even have forgiven me. But forgiving isn't forgetting."

"A woman who was still bitter about the past would avoid you. Instead, it's the other way around."

Raif turned to frown at Carrie. "Where did you get that notion? I was the one who asked Dorian to spend the day with me."

"How hard was it to convince her?"

"That doesn't prove anything. She was sick of cleaning closets."

"She could have gone shopping or visited with her friend."

Sudden excitement lit his face. "Out at the pond she *did...*" Carrie waited while Raif wrestled with his doubts. But then his expression hardened. "Forget it, Carrie. You're misinterpreting the facts."

"You and Dorian spent a long time alone together this afternoon," Carrie said shrewdly. "If you were indifferent to each other in that idyllic spot, then I guess I *am* wrong."

"I happen to know there is no man in Dorian's life right now. I think a lot of her, but I'm damned if I'll perform stud service!" Raif said violently.

Carrie's mouth thinned in annoyance. "There must be other men in Summerville who would be happy to oblige, assuming that's all she wants. Why would she waste time with you?"

"Maybe for old times' sake," he muttered.

"That must explain why you invited Sally and her husband for dinner. For old times' sake—and to save yourself the bother of going to pick Dorian up yourself."

"It only made good sense for her come with the Carters," he protested.

"If it makes sense to you, then I'm wasting my time," Carrie said disgustedly.

"Dorian didn't mind. I even asked her."

"What did you expect her to say? You didn't bother to look at her face or you might have a different opinion."

"You really think she was disappointed?" Raif asked slowly.

"In a lot of ways. Dorian won't be here much longer. If you're satisfied to let her walk out of your life again, then you did all the right things." Carrie picked up their cups and carried them to the sink. "I can't wait till the dishwasher is full so I can try it out."

"I think you'll see a difference," he answered absently.

Raif was preoccupied when he left the Center. Instead of going home, he drove in the opposite direction, away from town. The conversation with Carrie had shaken him, although he was convinced she was wrong. Dorian didn't want to renew their relationship. The only good memories she had of their short marriage were the times they made love.

Carrie couldn't guess just how magical those nights had been. Raif's groin still ached when he thought of Dorian's slender body beneath his. He would never forget the silky feeling of her skin, or her little cries of delight when he explored the secret spots that made her taut with desire.

That was the reason for the constant undercurrent of tension between them, not reawakened love. The potent attraction remained, even after all the other feelings were gone.

"At least I had sense enough not to do anything stupid," Raif gritted through his teeth.

God knew it wasn't easy. Today at the pond he had wanted to strip off that tiny suit and bury himself in Do-

rian's beautiful body. To make love to her for hours, with
infinite variety, the way they used to.

When Raif realized his foot was pressing the throttle almost to the floor, he slowed and turned into a country
lane. The peaceful sound of birds floated down from the
trees after he turned off the motor.

"Why the hell couldn't Carrie have left well enough
alone?" he groaned aloud.

He had been coping just fine until she raised hopes that
weren't justified. It was nonsense to think Dorian wanted
or needed anything from him. She was proud of her independence.

And yet... Raif stared through the windshield, a slight
frown puckering his brow. She had asked repeatedly for his
help when she could really have managed alone. And she'd
been upset when she'd misinterpreted the phone call he
received that night.

Growing excitement raced through Raif's veins as other
instances occurred to him. Could Carrie possibly be right?
If so, he was the biggest jackass God ever created!

Starting the motor with a roar, he drove onto the high-
way so fast the tires squealed. When he saw a gas station
at the edge of town, he pulled in abruptly and parked by a
telephone booth off to one side.

Dorian was peering listlessly into the refrigerator when
the phone rang. She answered it without enthusiasm, but
Raif's voice speeded up her heartbeat.

"Is anything wrong?" she asked uncertainly.

"Why would you think that?" His voice was buoyant.

"I just left you a short time ago."

"It was a nice day, wasn't it?"

That wasn't the word Dorian would have used, but she
said, "Yes, very nice. Did you fix Carrie's dishwasher?"

"I adjusted the thermostat. It should work better now."

"That's good." Dorian kept waiting to find out why he called.

Raif's voice was elaborately casual when he finally got to the point. "I've been having second thoughts about tomorrow night."

"You want to call it off?"

"On the contrary, I'm looking forward to it. I just decided it would be better if I picked you up instead of having the Carters do so."

What changed his mind? Dorian wondered. She wanted to believe it was because he felt the way she did, but that was wishful thinking. There was something fishy about this tardy change of plans.

"Why?" she asked suspiciously.

He hesitated. "We don't live that far from each other. It's no big deal to come and get you."

That occurred to you, or Carrie told you that you should? Dorian questioned silently. The older woman was a born matchmaker. Too bad her efforts were futile in this case. Raif probably gave in to get Carrie off his back. And because it wasn't that important one way or the other.

"So, is it still okay if I come a half hour earlier?" Raif asked.

"I'd really rather leave the arrangements the way they are, if you don't mind," Dorian answered matter-of-factly. "I can use that extra half hour to do things around here. I won't have unlimited time if those people who looked at the house make an offer. Wouldn't *that* be a stroke of luck?"

After a moment of silence, Raif said, "I hope it works out for you."

"I do, too," she replied with determined cheerfulness. "Maybe we'll have something to celebrate tomorrow night."

"I'll ice a bottle of champagne, just in case."

Raif's face was grim as he hung up the receiver and walked back to the truck. He climbed inside and banged the door with unnecessary force.

"So much for women's intuition," he muttered.

Chapter Seven

Dorian was ready when Sally rang the doorbell the next night, although it was only a quarter to seven.

"Don't panic," Sally said. "I know I'm early."

"That's okay, I'm all ready."

"You're going like that?" Sally looked her over critically.

Dorian glanced down at her white pants and flat shoes. "What's the matter with the way I look? I wore these pants to your house."

"That was a backyard barbecue," Sally answered dismissively.

"How do you know Raif isn't barbecuing?"

"Even if he is, it's a party, not just old friends getting together. I'll bet Carrie won't be wearing pants."

"I'm sure she won't mind if I do. Besides, I didn't bring anything dressy."

"You must have a skirt," Sally insisted.

"Nothing very special."

"Let's go upstairs and look in your closet." Sally started for the stairs.

Dorian followed, protesting all the way. "I don't see what difference it makes what I wear. I'm not trying to impress anyone."

"That's not the point. It's a simple matter of good manners." Sally opened Dorian's closet door and peered inside at the scant contents. "You do believe in traveling light, don't you?"

"I brought a couple of dresses, but something spilled on both of them. Come on, we've kept Ken waiting for nothing."

"He isn't ready yet. That's why I came over early, to visit with you." Sally took out a denim skirt, made a face and put it back. "Is this *all* you brought?"

"My ball gowns are at the cleaners," Dorian answered dryly.

Sally reached into a far corner of the closet and slid some hangers along the pole. "What are these?"

"I don't know. I haven't emptied this closet yet. Probably some things I left here on a long-ago visit."

"This is what I had in mind." Sally held up a cotton dress the color of sunshine. The bodice was held up by wide straps that crossed in front, and the full skirt flared out from a dropped waist. "This is perfect!"

"I'd forgotten all about that dress. It's years old."

"That doesn't matter. It's just right for an informal summer party."

Dorian smiled. "I guess that's why I left it here. Casual chic in L.A. is more apt to mean leather than linen."

"Try it on." Sally slipped the dress off the hanger and unzipped the back.

"I probably can't even fit into it after all this time," Dorian objected.

"Nonsense. You haven't gained a pound since I've known you."

"You mean I was a size six in kindergarten?"

"Stop wasting time," Sally ordered.

At her insistence, Dorian removed her blouse and pants, and stepped into the yellow dress.

"You'll have to take off your bra," Sally told her. "The straps will show."

"I don't have a strapless bra with me."

"So what? You don't need one."

"I don't know," Dorian said doubtfully.

"I'm surprised you even wear one. I thought you were a liberated woman." Sally tossed Dorian's bra on the bed, then zipped her up. "It fits perfectly. Turn around and let me see."

Dorian was gazing at her reflection in the mirror. She'd had a dress similar to this when she was married to Raif. Yellow had always been his favorite color on her. Would he think she was trying to stir up old memories? It was unlikely. Raif wouldn't remember a thing like that.

Sally interrupted her reverie. "*Now* you look better. Put on some high heels and you'll be all set. I know you have those with you. You were wearing them when you arrived."

"Are you sure I'm not overdressed?" Dorian asked hesitantly.

"You could wear that outfit during the day. It's a nice, simple summer dress," Sally assured her. When a horn honked outside, she said, "I'll go tell Kenny you'll be right down."

As she slipped into high-heeled white sandals, Dorian wondered how she'd let herself be talked into changing.

She'd been comfortable before; now the evening felt special. From sad experience, she knew that was an unreal expectation.

Sally brought Raif some chocolate-chip cookies she'd baked. "They aren't as elegant as your wine, but I hope you like them."

"They smell terrific. Do I have to serve them, or can I eat them all by myself?" he joked.

"I didn't think to bring you anything. I'm sorry," Dorian apologized.

"Your company is enough," Raif replied.

In the confusion of all the greetings, he hadn't taken a good look at her. Now he did. His eyes moved over her from the crown of her shining hair to her trim ankles.

"You look lovely," he said softly.

"Thank you," she murmured, hoping he wouldn't see how the small compliment pleased her.

"Didn't you have a dress like that once?"

"You remembered!" she exclaimed involuntarily.

Before he could respond, Ken said, "I'll be your bartender if you'll point me in the right direction."

Raif's face changed to a genial mask as he turned to his friend. "Tonight you're a guest. What can I fix for you and Sally?"

Carrie and Barnaby arrived a short time later. Raif made the introductions, and Ken and Sally acknowledged them politely, but they couldn't conceal their curiosity about the older man.

Barnaby wasn't at all disconcerted. "Were you part of the group of youngsters I chased off my property?" His eyes twinkled.

"I'm afraid so," Ken admitted.

"I hope you're not the kind that holds a grudge."

Ken grinned. "I hope you aren't either, sir."

"Not if you'll do me a favor."

"What is it?"

"Call me Barnaby. Sir makes me sound ancient, and I feel like a young man." He turned his head to smile at Carrie.

"You look like one." She returned his smile.

"Barnaby stays in shape by chopping wood." Dorian laughed as she retold the story of their meeting for Ken's benefit.

"I never knew I was that fascinating to women." Barnaby chuckled. "They couldn't take their eyes off me."

His lack of constraint put Ken and Sally at ease. They were soon talking animatedly with the older couple. When Raif went into the kitchen to fix drinks, Dorian followed him.

"Did you catch that little byplay between Carrie and Barnaby?" she asked. "It wouldn't surprise me if he proposed to her any day now."

Raif shrugged. "They aren't kids. What's the point in waiting around?"

"But they just met a few days ago. Don't you think they ought to get to know each other better before taking such a big step?"

Raif continued to drop ice cubes into a glass. "That's no guarantee of anything."

Dorian drew in her breath sharply. He didn't have to remind her of their own failure. She turned away without answering and started for the door, but Raif caught her arm.

He didn't pretend to have been making a general observation. "I'm sorry, Dorian. Forgive me?"

She gave him a brittle smile. "Why not? It's true."

"Maybe, but the time we had together was worth it. At least to me." He cupped her cheek in his palm.

Sally came into the kitchen. "Can I—" she stopped abruptly. "Oh, I'm sorry. I didn't mean to..." Her words trailed off.

Raif was unruffled. As his hand dropped to his side he asked pleasantly, "What can I get for you?"

"I just wondered if you needed any help."

Raif held out a glass. "You can take Carrie her drink, and tell Barnaby I haven't forgotten about him. His is coming up."

"I'll do it." Dorian reached for the glass before Sally could.

She needed to get away from Raif. That small caress meant nothing. He was only making amends for his callous remark, but even a meaningless caress made her melt like ice cream. This evening was going to be more difficult than she'd imagined.

Back in the kitchen, Sally remarked ruefully, "My timing was really rotten, wasn't it?"

"Not at all," Raif answered. "You didn't interrupt anything."

"That's not the way it looked."

"Appearances are deceiving."

"You two are the absolute limit!" she declared impatiently. "Anyone can see you still care about each other, but you won't admit it, and Dorian says it's all over between you."

"Believe her," Raif said curtly. He put Barnaby's drink on a tray and carried it into the living room.

"That cheese is delicious," Carrie told him, gesturing toward the coffee table where a plate held crackers and a wedge of brie.

"I'm glad you like it," he replied. "I didn't make a lot of hors d'oeuvres because I wanted you to save your appetite for dinner."

"Whatever Raif's serving is bound to be delicious," Dorian said.

"You'd better not rely too heavily on her recommendation. Dorian thinks frozen dinners are haute cuisine," he teased.

"I never said they were good, I only said they were fast and filling," she answered.

"That's a sad commentary on modern life," Barnaby remarked. "Next, I suppose we'll have little pills you can take three times a day instead of meals."

"Think of all the time that would save," Dorian said.

"And the money you could make marketing them." Ken sighed. "That's the kind of idea I'm looking for."

"Are you an inventor?" Barnaby asked.

"No, just a working stiff. At least, at the moment."

"I love this room, Raif," Sally commented quickly. "Dorian said you refurnished the whole place."

"My parents did. I merely made a few structural changes."

"He's being modest," Dorian said. "Raif has done wonderful things here. You should have seen the place before. It was—" Her cheeks flushed as she stumbled to a halt.

"A dump," Raif finished calmly.

"That wasn't what I was going to say." Dorian felt terrible, knowing he wasn't fooled. In her admiration for his work she'd gotten carried away.

"It's all right, honey," he soothed. "That's what it was. My parents couldn't afford to fix it up. I was the kid from the wrong side of the tracks," he explained to Carrie and Barnaby.

"Nobody ever thought of you that way," Ken protested.

"He was the most popular boy in town," Sally told the older couple.

"That's laying it on a little thick," Raif said wryly.

"It's true," Dorian chimed in. "You won a full scholarship to college."

He grinned. "That proves I was smart, not popular."

"I'm sure you were both," Carrie said diplomatically. "I never knew your mother, but a lot of the women at the Center did. They have only flattering things to say about her."

"She's a nice person," Raif said fondly.

"Did they move away for business reasons?" Barnaby asked.

"No, they always wanted to live near the water, so they bought a home in Laguna." Raif named a resort town on the California coast.

"I gather your father is retired."

"Yes, he made a good investment many years ago, and it finally paid off." Raif seemed amused by a private joke.

"My situation is just the opposite," Barnaby remarked. "I've been retired for so many years that I wouldn't mind getting back into business."

"What kind of work did you do?" Sally asked.

"Investment banking. Not very interesting, I'm afraid. I'd prefer something with a more hands-on approach."

Raif gazed at him speculatively. "The ideal situation would be to combine the two."

"Do you have anything specific in mind?" the older man asked.

"I might. Remember that tract of land I mentioned to you?"

"The one adjoining my property? I don't have the expertise to handle anything of the magnitude you proposed."

"We'll discuss it. Some other time," Raif added smoothly.

The conversation drifted to a different subject, but Dorian didn't take part. Was Raif trying to get backing from Barnaby to start his own construction company? While she welcomed this show of ambition, it seemed slightly underhanded to cultivate a man socially for business purposes. Especially a man like Barnaby. He'd been out of the mainstream for so long that he must be unsophisticated about financial matters. Was that what Raif was counting on?

As Dorian glanced over at his handsome, laughing face, she knew her suspicions were unworthy. Raif had never taken advantage of anyone when she knew him, and he couldn't have changed that drastically. She refused to let the little seed of doubt take root.

Raif's dinner was as delicious as Dorian had predicted. He served a crown of lamb with new potatoes and baby green peas. The platter was garnished with parsley and little cherry tomatoes, and could have graced the pages of a gourmet magazine.

They all complimented him on his superb cooking, proving their sincerity by taking second helpings.

Raif had refused assistance in serving the meal, but when it was time for dessert, the women insisted on clearing the table.

"You should see that kitchen," Sally told Ken when they were seated again.

"It has every modern gadget you could wish for," Carrie declared.

"To really appreciate what Raif did in there, you'd have to know what it looked like before," Dorian said. "Do you have any pictures?" she asked him.

He shook his head. "I'm afraid not."

"That's too bad," Sally said. "I love those before and after photographs in magazines."

"That reminds me of something I've been meaning to tell you," Raif said to Dorian. "I ran across some old snapshots of your parents."

"Oh, Raif, I'd love to see them! Where were they taken?"

He hesitated for a moment. "At your house. After our wedding rehearsal."

"I remember that night!" Sally exclaimed. "We all went back to Dorrie's house and partied till the wee hours. Your parents said you and Raif would look terrible the next day if you didn't get some sleep, but we were all having such a good time we didn't want to leave."

"I remember," Dorian said softly, her eyes meeting Raif's.

"Show us the pictures," Sally urged. "I want to see what I looked like with a waistline."

"At least you'll get yours back." Ken patted his middle. "I've gained ten pounds since those days."

"That's just a sign of maturity," Carrie consoled him.

"Then how come I'm more mature than Barnaby?" Ken laughed, eyeing the older man's flat midsection.

"Don't worry, there's just more of you to love," Sally said fondly. "Get the pictures, Raif."

"Not now," he answered. "Carrie and Barnaby wouldn't be interested."

"We wouldn't mind," Barnaby said politely.

"No, Raif is right," Ken said. "We brought out the old album at our house the other night, and reminisced for hours."

"I'll give them to you before you leave," Raif promised Dorian. He glanced around the table. "If everyone is finished with dessert, let's take our coffee into the living room."

The evening passed so pleasantly that they weren't aware of the time until Ken smothered a yawn. "I'm sorry," he apologized, "but I've been up since six o'clock."

Carrie consulted her watch. "My goodness, it's almost eleven."

"Yes, we really must leave, but the rest of you don't have to," Sally said. "Could you drop Dorrie off, Raif?"

"I'd be happy to take both of you home if you'd like to stay," Barnaby offered.

"Thanks, but I'll go with Kenny," Sally said. "Your dinner was fantastic, Raif."

After they left, the two remaining couples discussed a variety of subjects, from world events to local happenings. All four were well-informed people, so the conversation was stimulating.

Finally, however, Barnaby said, "This has been delightful, but it's time we left, too. Are you ready, Dorian?"

"Whenever you are," she answered. "May I have the snapshots, Raif?"

"I'm glad you reminded me. They're out in the storeroom, though. It might take a few minutes. Do you mind waiting?" he asked Barnaby.

"You probably want to look at them together," Carrie said before Barnaby had a chance to answer. "Why don't we go on, and let you take Dorian home?" she asked smoothly.

"I can get them some other time," Dorian said hastily. "It's silly for Raif to have to go out at this hour."

"No problem," he assured her. "I'd like to look at those old photos again, myself."

"We'll leave you, then." Carrie overrode Dorian's sputtering objections. "Thanks for a wonderful evening, Raif."

When he and Dorian were alone, Raif said, "Pour yourself another cup of coffee. I'll be back in a jiffy."

He didn't seem at all constrained at being alone with her, but Dorian couldn't sit still. As soon as he left the room she went into the kitchen.

They had put away the food, but that was all Raif would permit them to do. Stacks of dirty dishes still cluttered the counters. Dorian placed them in the sink and ran hot water over them.

"You shouldn't be doing that," Raif scolded when he came into the kitchen and found her. "You'll get your pretty dress dirty."

"It's washable," she answered dismissively. "You can't go to bed and leave this mess."

"I'll clean up after I take you home."

"I'll leave the pots for you," she promised. "Bring in the dessert plates while I load the dishwasher."

Dorian's helpfulness was only partly altruistic. She felt less self-conscious with Raif when she was too busy to look at him.

After the kitchen was reasonably clean, Raif said, "Okay, now we can get to the pictures." His gaze sharpened as he glanced at her. "I knew it! You got something on your dress."

Looking down to inspect herself, she noticed a small brown stain on her midriff. "It's just a little spot. It will wash out."

"If that's coffee, you'd better get it out now before it sets permanently."

Raif dampened a paper towel with cold water. Bracing her with an arm around her back, he rubbed the small spot vigorously. Her skin tingled under the thin fabric, and Dorian was acutely conscious of the fact she wasn't wearing a bra.

"There, I got it out," Raif said with a final pat.

"That's good," she murmured in relief.

He glanced up at her barely audible response. Suddenly Raif realized he was holding her in his arms. For one electric moment his embrace tightened and they stared at each other. Dorian made a tiny sound—a protest or a plea? She wasn't sure. It broke the spell, however. Raif released her and crushed the paper towel in his big hand, clenching his fingers.

That was the only sign of stress. His voice was normal as he said, "Thanks for the help. Now we can finally look at those snapshots."

Dorian's nerves were coiled tightly as she sat next to Raif on the couch. But the vintage pictures of her parents soon drove everything else out of her mind.

"They look so happy," she remarked poignantly.

Raif could see the sadness in Dorian's eyes. He tried to tease her out of her melancholy. "Why shouldn't they have been happy? They finally had hopes of getting to use their own telephone again."

Dorian couldn't help laughing. "Dad used to say the only way *he* could get a message was by carrier pigeon."

They pored over the snapshots together, commenting on old friends who had been present that night. But Dorian's attention was centered on her parents.

"I'm so glad you found these photos, Raif. They bring Mother and Dad back so vividly. I can almost imagine they're just off on vacation."

"You have to let go, honey," he said gently.

"That isn't easy," she answered in a lost little voice. "I miss them so."

"I know." He took her in his arms and guided her head to his shoulder.

"I thought I was so strong. I've always been able to stand up to anything until now." Her muffled voice was thick with tears.

"You're doing fine," he soothed, kissing her hair lightly. "I'm proud of you."

"When will it stop hurting so much, Raif?" she asked like a child.

"Time eases the pain." His eyes were bleak as he smoothed her hair.

"I missed you at the funeral," she murmured.

"I didn't hear about it until later. I was out of the country."

"I'm glad that was the reason," she said simply.

Raif lifted her chin so he could look at her. "Didn't you know I would have been there if I'd known?"

"I was afraid maybe you thought I didn't want you."

"I would have taken that chance," he said tenderly.

"You're a very nice human being." The need to touch him overwhelmed Dorian. She reached up and trailed her fingers across his cheek.

Raif's eyes darkened to jade green as he lowered his head, almost in slow motion. Dorian could have turned her face away, but she didn't. Their lips barely touched at first. She was more conscious of the warmth of his breath mingling with hers.

Then the pressure of his lips increased and he curled his hand around the nape of her neck, immobilizing her needlessly. Dorian's lips parted willingly. She returned his kisses with pent-up hunger, twining her fingers through his hair.

It was as though a dam had burst for both of them. Restraint and denial were swept away in a hot tide of passion that could no longer be ignored.

"This is what I've dreamed about night after night." Raif's hands moved restlessly over her back. "I never got over wanting you."

"I couldn't forget, either," she whispered.

Dorian traced the taut muscles that strained to hold her closer. The years fell away and they belonged to each other once more. She had the right to slide her hands inside his waistband, to explore every area of his splendid body.

His long frame became rigid under her questing fingers. "I never wanted to forget our nights together, even when the memories drove me crazy, like you're doing now."

His mouth possessed hers with such intensity that her breath was almost sucked away. The deep probing kiss made her taut with desire. Dorian quivered as one of Raif's hands moved to cup her breast. The thin barrier of her dress only heightened the sensuous feeling.

When he discovered she wasn't wearing a bra, a low groan of satisfaction rumbled in his throat. His thumb circled her nipple, sending jagged flashes of pleasure through her. The pink tip stiffened and became exquisitely sensitive. When Raif removed his hand, she uttered a tiny cry of protest.

Reassurance came as he slid her zipper to her waist. His eyes glowed like live coals as he guided the wide straps off her shoulders and watched her dress slither down. It caught on the points of her breasts, exposing half circles of deep coral.

Raif lowered his head to brush his lips over the rosy aureoles, and the dress slipped to her waist. He cupped both breasts in his hand while he kissed one rosette, then the other.

"You're more beautiful than before," he said huskily. "How is that possible?"

"I haven't changed," she answered faintly. "You still make me feel the same."

He gazed into her eyes as he urged her gently onto the cushions. Poised over her, he murmured, "Do you want me as much as I want you?"

"Maybe more." She reached up to unbutton his shirt.

He shrugged it off his shoulders and clasped her in his arms. The sensation was inexpressible. She moved against his bare chest, feeling liquid fire race through her veins. The excitement mounted when Raif lifted her from the couch and carried her into the bedroom. No words were necessary. They both knew that what was was about to happen was inevitable.

The room was lit only by moonlight. He stood her on her feet and unfastened the remaining part of her zipper. The loosened dress slid to the floor and she stepped out of it. In the dim light, Raif's hands looked very brown against her white skin as he rolled her pantyhose down her hips.

He knelt before her and paused to dip his tongue into her navel. Then his lips trailed down her stomach, scorching a fiery path. Dorian gasped when he stopped at the juncture of her thighs and lingered.

She anchored her fingers in his thick hair because her legs felt boneless. "Raif, please," she begged.

"That's what I want to do, darling—please you." His eyes were brilliant as he gazed up at her. "I want to bring you more pleasure than you've ever known."

"You always did," she said with a sigh, sinking down onto the bed.

Raif stripped off his clothes and covered her body with his. The hard contact sent a shock of awareness through Dorian. She arched her hips and reached for him blindly.

"I need you so," she pleaded.

"I've waited so long to hear you say that," he said exultantly.

Parting her legs, he plunged deeply, filling her with joy. Thrust after thrust intensified the sensation. Their bodies rocked together and then parted, but only for an instant. They were bonded to each other, joined in a shared rapture almost too intense to endure. The glorious, throbbing climax sent golden rays of pleasure radiating through their taut bodies.

Afterward they relaxed in each other's arms, utterly fulfilled. Both were too content to stir for a long time. Finally, Raif reached up to stroke Dorian's hair languidly.

"Do you feel as fantastic as I do?" he asked.

She smiled blissfully. "If everyone felt this good there'd be a tax on it."

Raif propped himself up on one elbow to gaze down at her. "It isn't over, is it, Dorian?"

Her heart lurched. What was Raif suggesting? She laughed breathlessly. "Are you asking me to spend the night?"

"I insist on it." He kissed the tip of her nose.

"That's good. I don't like to sleep alone."

"What makes you think you're going to get any sleep?" he teased.

She wriggled seductively. "I can do that anytime."

"Not when I'm around."

"You're not around all the time." If Raif needed an opening, she'd provided him with a perfect one.

He didn't seize the opportunity. "I'd like to be, but Sally watches our every move." He laughed.

"She'd feel terrible if she knew she inhibited you," Dorian said lightly. "Sally would like to see us get together again."

"So would Carrie."

"Did you tell her about us?" Dorian asked in surprise.

"Only that we'd been married at one time. Actually, I wasn't the one who told her. It's common knowledge."

"What did Carrie say to you?" Dorian asked casually.

"We talked about living alone," Raif answered vaguely. "She said it was lonely."

"Any woman could solve that problem for you. What makes you think Carrie picked me?"

"She admires you. So do I." He smiled fondly.

Dorian had trouble hiding her disappointment. Was Raif that obtuse, or was he being purposely evasive? She had to find out, even at the cost of her pride.

"Is that what you feel for me...admiration?" she asked slowly.

He framed his answer carefully. "I think we share the same feeling for each other that we always did."

"You mean physically? Is that why you married me, Raif?"

His eyes were shadowed. "You still have doubts about me, don't you?"

"No! I shouldn't have asked that. No two people were more in love than we were. I guess I just wanted to hear you say it," she finished wistfully.

"All right. I married you because I loved you," he said evenly. "Do you believe me?"

"Yes."

"Then do you still think I wanted out of our marriage because I couldn't handle the responsibilities that came with it?"

Raif deserved a truthful answer. Any chance for their future happiness depended on complete honesty. As Dorian looked back on her behavior in those early days, she realized that, emotionally she'd been a little girl playing house. That wasn't to say she didn't love Raif; merely that she wasn't ready for marriage.

His expression hardened when she didn't reply immediately. "That's okay, Dorian. It's all past and done with anyway. I don't know why I brought it up."

"Let me answer your question, Raif."

"I'd rather you didn't. Unlike you, I don't want to hear you say it."

She was near tears at the coldness in his voice. Why did things always go wrong between them? "I didn't think we'd argue tonight," she faltered.

His mouth twisted wryly. "We're only tiptoeing around the edges of an argument. This is pallid compared to some of the ones we've had."

"I don't want to argue anymore, Raif," she said sadly.

"Not when we have better things to do," he agreed. His teeth nibbled delicately on her ear, and his hand glided across her stomach.

Dorian knew she should stop him. She'd told herself this wasn't enough. But when Raif touched her the way he was doing now, nothing else seemed to matter.

Her lips parted for the invasion of his tongue, and her body moved restlessly in anticipation. She ran her hands over his lithe body, savoring the hard male feel of him. When he drew in his breath sharply and scissored his legs around hers, Dorian dug her fingers into the bunched muscles of his buttocks in an effort to draw him closer.

Their hips met and fused as they merged into one person. The shared ecstasy pounded through their joined bodies and erupted at the same time. Even their hearts beat in rhythm and slowed together.

In the aftermath they were both cautious, murmuring only tender endearments. Dorian couldn't ask for more. Not now. She didn't want anything to spoil this perfect night.

And it *was* perfect. They drifted off to sleep in each other's arms, and awoke with renewed hunger. Raif satisfied her so completely that she knew he must feel something for her. Everything was going to work out.

Sunlight streaming through the window woke Dorian the next morning. She opened her eyes to find Raif staring at her. His somber expression changed so swiftly that she was sure she'd imagined it. He was smiling as he leaned over to kiss her.

"I thought you were going to sleep all day," he teased.

She glanced over at the clock. "It's only six in the morning!"

"That's the best time of day. We should be out jogging."

Dorian turned on her stomach and put a pillow over her head. "Wake me when you get back."

"Don't you do anything healthy? You need more exercise."

"I got enough last night," she answered in a muffled voice.

He chuckled richly, stroking her bare bottom. "Do you have a problem with that? I do the work over, when I have complaints."

"Work?" She turned over and hit him with the pillow.

He fended her off, laughing. "Okay, I give repeat performances. Is that better?"

"You'll be lucky if I even speak to you again." She pretended outrage.

"I hope to do a lot more than that," he murmured, taking her in his arms.

"I really should go home, Raif," she said without conviction.

"Why?"

"Because Sally will be calling to discuss the party. If I'm not there this early in the morning, she might guess I didn't come home all night. You know how Sally is. I don't want to get her hopes up." Dorian held her breath, waiting for Raif to say he shared the same hopes as Sally.

Instead, he released her reluctantly. "At least let me make you breakfast."

Dorian couldn't believe his response. She got out of bed quickly before Raif could see her face. "I told you, I don't eat breakfast. I'll just take a fast shower."

When she came out of the bathroom, the appetizing smell of bacon and eggs greeted her. "I'm not going to eat them," she muttered, although they smelled wonderful.

"You're just in time." Raif smiled when she came into the kitchen.

"Don't you listen to anything I say?" she scolded as he held a chair for her.

"Only when it's something I want to hear," he answered cheerfully.

"You've demonstrated that."

"You're only grumpy because you're hungry," he soothed.

"I am *not* grumpy. I simply object to being treated like a child."

Raif grinned. "That's the last thing I expected you to accuse me of."

"Don't be lewd."

"I'm counting my blessings," he said huskily, taking her hand and kissing the palm.

Her fingers curled, as though protecting something precious. "Oh, Raif, what am I going to do with you?"

"Eat your bacon and eggs, and then we'll see if we can think of something."

Dorian couldn't stay angry at Raif for long. He bewildered and aggravated her, but he also filled her to the brim with happiness. She decided to stop trying to figure him out, and simply enjoy him. Sooner or later she'd break down his resistance.

Chapter Eight

The telephone was ringing when Raif returned from taking Dorian home after breakfast.

"I was about to hang up," Carrie said. "I hope I didn't take you away from anything."

"No, I just got back from . . . doing an errand."

"You get out early," she commented. "Anyway, I'm glad I caught you. I want to thank you for a really delightful evening."

"I enjoyed having you," Raif answered courteously.

"Barnaby and I both had such a good time, and your dinner was delicious. I'd like to return your hospitality, but my cooking can't compare to yours."

"Don't think I'm going to let you off the hook with *that* lame excuse," he teased.

"I was afraid I wouldn't get away with it." Carrie laughed. "All right, I'll check with Barnaby, and we'll make a date."

"Anytime."

"Did you and Dorian enjoy looking at the snapshots after we left?" Carrie asked casually.

"It was a little traumatic for her, but I think she was glad to see them."

"Poor thing. It must be very difficult, being all alone in the world."

Raif sighed. "You're not going to start that again, Carrie?"

"Not at all. It was a very recent tragedy. I was simply remarking on how sad she must be."

"She is. Dorian gives the impression of being completely self-sufficient, but she's feeling a little lost right now."

"Who wouldn't? Everyone needs someone they can depend on."

Raif laughed harshly. "Meaning me? Forget it, Carrie! I found out last night that Dorian and I have no future together."

"You argued after we left?" Carrie asked hesitantly.

"No, we didn't argue." Raif's voice softened, then firmed once more. "We had a frank talk, and I discovered what I've known all along. Dorian still feels I failed her. I can't spend the rest of my life under a cloud, even if I were guilty as charged."

"I'm so sorry," Carrie said helplessly. "I wouldn't expect that of Dorian. Are you sure you didn't misunderstand her?"

"I asked her a direct question," he answered bleakly.

She sighed. "I guess I just wanted you both to be happy."

"Face it, Carrie. You're a lousy matchmaker." Raif made a heavy attempt at humor. "If you want to play Cupid, aim your darts at Barnaby. You two seemed very compatible last night.''

"He's a wonderful man, Raif,'' she said softly.

"I agree. Don't let him get away.''

"I don't intend to.'' She laughed. "I hope to snap him up before the competition gets a chance at him.''

"He couldn't do better than you,'' Raif assured her fondly. "You've shown him there's a whole world out there.''

"You helped. Barnaby was very interested in your idea for developing the property next to his.''

"I must admit I was rather surprised at his reaction. I thought he might object.''

"Just the opposite. He wants to talk to you about getting involved in the project. Was that just a notion you had, or is someone really interested in going ahead with the plan?''

"Someone is definitely interested. There's a meeting this afternoon with the owner of the acreage.''

"Are you looking for investors?''

"Not really, but if Barnaby wants to work, that might make a difference.''

"I think that's the part that excited him. He's too vital a man to sit around and vegetate the way he's been doing. All that pent-up energy needs an outlet.''

"You might have competition from a different source,'' Raif warned.

"I don't want to take him from one isolation chamber to another,'' she answered simply.

"You're a very rare lady, Carrie,'' Raif said admiringly.

"Not really. Most women want the people they care about to be happy. Will you put in a good word for Barnaby?''

"Consider it done."

Carrie must have phoned Barnaby as soon as she hung up, because he called Raif a short time later. After a few minutes of preliminary chitchat, Barnaby got to the point.

"I'm interested in hearing more about that housing development. You said we'd talk about it."

"Just how involved do you want to get?" Raif asked.

"I'm a banker. Or at least I was. Naturally I'd have to go over the plans and see some figures before I committed any sizeable amount."

"Spoken like a true financier." Raif chuckled. "You haven't lost your touch, Barnaby."

"I've led a sheltered life these last years, but I'm not senile," the older man answered dryly.

"I'm glad to hear it, but I'm afraid I gave you the wrong impression. The developer isn't looking for capital."

"But you just asked me how much I'd be willing to invest."

"No, I asked if you'd be willing to work."

"That's the whole idea! If there was anything I could do. I'm not young enough to put in eight hours a day at manual labor, and the only thing I know about building houses is how they're financed." Barnaby's initial eagerness changed to dejection.

"Workmen are easy to find. A man of your expertise could be useful in the management end."

"Pencil pushing?" Barnaby asked skeptically.

"Not entirely. You'd be required to make on-site inspections and confer with the foremen."

"That's more like it! Where do I go to apply for the job?"

"You're a little premature." Raif laughed. "The deal on the property hasn't gone through yet."

"Could I meet with the principals?"

Raif hesitated. "There isn't any hurry. Construction can't begin until escrow is closed."

"I'd really like to meet these people before they start putting together their organization. Timing is everything."

"I guarantee you'll be considered, Barnaby."

"I'm sure you'll do your best, Raif, but I don't want to put you on the spot. Maybe they'll think I'm too old for the job. If that's the case, I'd prefer to know about it right away. I don't want to get my hopes up for nothing."

"This really means a lot to you, doesn't it?" Raif asked slowly.

"It's a road map to a normal life again," the other man answered quietly.

Raif was silent for a long moment. "We have to talk, Barnaby. I'll come to your place this afternoon."

After Raif brought her home that morning, Dorian changed into her work clothes, the usual jeans and a T-shirt. The closets were emptied, except for her own, and the knickknacks had all been packed away. She was almost finished except for the attic and basement, the worst jobs.

Those were the places where she really could use Raif's help, but he hadn't offered. When he dropped her off, he didn't even mention seeing her again. He simply took it for granted that they'd get together later on, Dorian assured herself. How could she doubt it after last night?

A slight feeling of uneasiness plagued her, however. Wouldn't you think he'd have said *something?* She drifted through the downstairs rooms, unable to settle down to anything. When the doorbell rang, her heart lifted.

The real estate agent was standing on the doorstep with a man and a woman. "Oh, you're home, Miss Merrill,"

John Saputo, the agent said. "I thought I'd better check before I used my key. I called early this morning and there was no answer."

"I must have been in the shower," Dorian said.

"I thought that might be it. This is Mr. and Mrs. Bronwyn. I brought them here the other day, and they'd like to take another look at your house."

"Please come in." Dorian opened the door wide.

"I don't know if you noticed the size of this entry the last time," the agent remarked to his clients, exuding enthusiasm. "They don't build houses like this anymore."

They answered in noncommittal grunts, gazing around critically.

"I'll get out of your way," Dorian said, unwilling to hear the negative comments she was sure were forthcoming.

She couldn't stay away from the Bronwyns, however. They were all over the house, appearing in every room she sought refuge in. Finally Dorian gave up.

"I have some errands to do," she told the agent. "Stay as long as you like. Just lock up when you leave."

He lowered his voice confidentially. "I'll phone you later—with good news, I hope. These people are really interested."

"You must be mistaken. They don't seem to like the house one bit."

He winked at her. "That's how I can tell."

Dorian drove around aimlessly for a while before deciding to visit Carrie. She was probably deep in plans for the youth project, and might welcome some help with them.

Inside, the Center was as quiet as it had been the first time Dorian went there with Raif. The same group of comatose people were staring silently at the flickering television screen where a manic emcee asked silly questions. But live voices filtered in from outside.

A group of women were gardening in the backyard. Some were pruning overgrown bushes, while others planted flowers. Motivated by Carrie, no doubt. Dorian joined them and looked around for her friend.

"Carrie left after lunch," a woman named Lillian told her. Dorian recognized her as one of the members who had helped at the bake sale. "She won't be back today."

"I'm sorry I missed her." Dorian's disappointment was evident.

"You can catch her at home. She said she had things to do."

"Then I won't disturb her."

"Don't worry about it. Carrie is always glad to have people drop by. You can give her a message and save me a phone call. Tell her the man from Marten's Department Store called to say the VCR will be delivered tomorrow."

"I'm not really a close friend of Carrie's," Dorian said hesitantly. "I don't even know where she lives."

"Right near here in the Sunnydale District." Lillian gave her the address.

Carrie's house was attractive and well kept up, like its owner. Pink geraniums lined the walk, and roses climbed a trellis almost to the cedar shake roof. It wasn't a large house, but it looked hospitable. Stereo music, mixed with the sound of a washing machine in use, came from the open window.

Carrie opened the door in answer to Dorian's ring. "Well, this is a nice surprise."

"I hope I'm not interrupting anything. Lillian said you wouldn't mind."

"She was right. I'm just catching up on a few necessary, but boring, things like the laundry. Come on in. Did you want to see me about something, or were you simply in the neighborhood?"

"I'm a displaced person." Dorian laughed. "Mr. Saputo brought a couple to see my house, and I didn't have anyplace to put myself."

"At least you're starting to get some action."

"I'm not too optimistic about these prospects. They turned up their noses at everything, from the minute they walked through the door."

"That's a good sign."

"John said the same thing, but I don't understand your reasoning."

"It means they're preparing to offer less than you're asking by pointing out all the unfavorable aspects."

"I suppose that's logical, but I didn't care much for them."

"This is business, not friendship," Carrie replied crisply. "The real estate agent undoubtedly told them your situation, and they're hoping your price isn't firm."

"I put a fair price on the house," Dorian objected. "I didn't try to get top dollar."

"Even so, the market is soft right now. You might have to wait around for a while. It depends on how anxious you are to sell."

"I can afford to wait," Dorian said slowly. "The upkeep is minimal. I can't stay here indefinitely, though."

"I imagine you're anxious to get back to Los Angeles."

Dorian stirred restlessly in her chair. "I am, and I'm not."

"You can't have it both ways," Carrie said evenly.

"I discovered that a long time ago," Dorian answered soberly.

"Well, if your house is sold, the decisions will be made for you. There won't be anything to keep you here."

"I guess that's true." After a moment, Dorian forced a smile. "This isn't getting your laundry done. I'd better let you go back to work."

Carrie's rather stern expression softened as she gazed at the younger woman's forlorn face. "Don't rush off. Come in the kitchen and keep me company while I put the clothes in the dryer."

Dorian went along with the suggestion because she didn't want to go home and listen for the telephone to ring. Her earlier insecurity was heightened by Carrie's assumption that there was nothing between her and Raif. That information could only have come from him, when Carrie was trying to get them back together. But that was before last night, Dorian insisted to herself.

Carrie made coffee and they sat at the kitchen table and talked about the dinner at Raif's the night before.

"Is there anything that man can't do?" Carrie asked. "He continually surprises me."

"Me, too," Dorian said.

Carrie slanted a glance at her. "I imagine Raif has changed since you were married."

"In many ways." Dorian played with a cookie crumb. "I don't know how he feels anymore. About things," she added hastily.

"He wasn't overjoyed to find out *you* haven't changed your belief," Carrie observed acidly.

"About what?" Dorian looked at her in bewilderment.

"I shouldn't have said that. It's none of my business."

"But what did you mean?"

"It isn't important. Please forget the whole thing. I'm really fond of both of you," Carrie said earnestly.

Dorian would have questioned her further, but the doorbell rang. When Carrie went to answer it, Dorian heard male voices. After a few moments, Raif and Barnaby followed Carrie into the kitchen.

"I told them to come in here so you could hear the good news, too," Carrie said. "Barnaby has a job!"

"Congratulations," Dorian said. "Doing what?"

"I owe it all to Raif." His face was animated. "I'm going to be a supervisor on the housing project that's going up next to me. I might even become a limited partner if they'll let me invest."

"If they'll let you?" Carrie asked.

"This is a company that doesn't need money. It would be strictly a favor. That's one thing that stops me. I wouldn't want to take advantage of anyone."

"Any venture is a risk," Raid said easily. "Take your time before you make up your mind."

Dorian's heart sank as she gazed at his smiling face. That sounded uncomfortably like a confidence man's pitch. Warn the sucker off something, and he'll beg you to take his money. But Raif wouldn't stoop to such a trick. How could it even cross her mind? Still, the subject had only been mentioned in passing last night, and now it was almost an accomplished fact.

Raif's expression changed as he glanced over and met her eyes. "I didn't expect to see you here," he said softly.

"I didn't know if I'd see you at all today," she said, searching for some clue.

Before he could answer, Carrie announced, "This has been an eventful day. Barnaby got a job, and Dorian may have sold her house."

Raif's face became impassive. "That means you'll be leaving soon," he said to Dorian.

"I don't have an offer yet. Carrie and the real estate agent are the confident ones."

"I'd bet on it, from what you told me," Carrie said.

"Keep a good thought," Raif told Dorian. "You might get lucky."

"This calls for a celebration," Carrie declared. "I have a bottle of champagne I've been saving for a special occasion, and I can't think of a better one."

Dorian had never felt *less* like celebrating. She no longer had to wonder about Raif's feelings. He was letting her go without a word of regret. Her grandiose plans for their future together seemed downright laughable. Except that Dorian felt more like crying.

"Let's have a party," Carrie suggested. "After we drink a toast we'll get take-out chicken and have dinner here."

"I have a better idea," Barnaby said. "I'll take everybody out to dinner. How about it, Raif? Dorian?"

"Either one is all right with me," Raif answered.

"I think an impromptu evening here would be more fun," Carrie said. "You're the deciding vote, Dorian, since Raif doesn't have a preference."

Dorian was too devastated to get through an evening without revealing her emotions. "I can't join you," she said. "I have to go home."

"If you're worried about missing a call from the realtor, you can phone him from here," Carrie said.

"Deals aren't closed that rapidly," Barnaby assured her.

"It isn't only that," Dorian answered desperately. "If there's a chance that a sale is pending, I still have two very dirty jobs to do."

"I'll help you with them tomorrow," Raif promised.

Now that he thought her departure was imminent, he wasn't worried about getting too involved. "You've done enough for me," she answered with dignity.

"You two decide," Raif said. "I want to talk to Dorian."

He took her hand and led her into the backyard. In the gathering darkness, all the flowers were pastel. The scent of jasmine would always remind Dorian of that evening, and Raif's strong hands clasping her shoulders.

"Please stay," he said urgently.

"What's the point, Raif? To keep up appearances? You didn't intend to see me again, did you?"

"Why do you say that?" he asked, but his eyes didn't meet hers.

"Because it's true, although I honestly don't know why. I thought last night was very special, but evidently not to you."

"You're wrong!" He crushed her in his arms and buried his face in her hair. "It was more than I could ever have hoped for."

"But not an experience you cared to repeat," she said bitterly. "I'm really dense. When you said goodbye, it took me a while to realize you meant for good."

"You're putting words in my mouth," he protested.

"Did you intend to see me again, Raif?" she asked evenly.

He stared at her searchingly, as though memorizing her features. "I don't have any choice," he answered huskily. "I couldn't stay away from you if I wanted to. Not even if I thought it was best for both of us. I would have been outside your window tonight, throwing pebbles to wake you up."

His mouth closed over hers in a kiss that was almost desperate with hunger. Something about his passionate words was disturbing, but Dorian wasn't in a mood to examine them. She was too relieved to have her doubts erased. Raif's ardor couldn't be questioned. They clung to each other as though they'd been separated for weeks instead of hours.

Finally Dorian reluctantly drew away. "They're waiting for us. We should go inside."

Raif chuckled deeply. "I have a much better idea."

Bubbles of sheer happiness coursed through Dorian's veins. "Can you hang on to it for a while? All of a sudden I'm starving."

"You're no fun," he grumbled.

She smiled enchantingly. "I'll remind you of that later."

Barnaby handed them each a glass of champagne when they went inside. "What did you decide?" he asked.

Carrie laughed. "I don't think they were discussing dinner, Barnaby. I guess it's up to us. Let's flip a coin."

Carrie won the toss, and the men went out to get fried chicken. While they were gone, the two women set the table and tossed a salad.

It was a delightful evening, although different from the one the night before. They sat around the kitchen table eating fried chicken and wiping their fingers on paper napkins.

"What must you think of me?" Carrie lamented. "Barnaby gave us an elegant lunch, and Raif served a gourmet dinner."

"Think how I feel," Dorian said. "I haven't had you over for anything."

"I'm available for breakfast," Barnaby joked.

"Don't expect too much," Raif warned. "All you'll get is a cup of black coffee."

"Are you one of those people like me who skip breakfast?" Carrie asked her.

"Unless she's coerced," Raif grinned.

"Don't be too hard on her. It's no fun to eat alone," Barnaby said.

"Every person who's single knows that," Carrie agreed. "Even when my husband propped the newspaper between us, I knew he was there." She smiled wryly. "I've considered getting a dog and teaching him to sit on a chair across from me so I can hear breathing."

Barnaby took her hand. "Breathing is one of my talents. Will I do?"

"Are you serious?" she asked uncertainly.

"I'm asking you to marry me. I realize this isn't exactly a romantic moment, and you might think it's too soon. But we've spent all our time together since we met. Actually, we've gotten to know each other better than old friends who only see each other occasionally." His words came tumbling out as if to silence her objections before she voiced them.

Carrie laughed breathlessly. "You don't have to convince me. I accept with great pleasure."

After the general rejoicing and congratulations, Raif joked, "I have only one question to ask, Barnaby. What took you so long to propose?"

"I was unemployed." The older man's eyes twinkled. "How could I ask Carrie to marry a man who didn't have a job?"

A light bulb went on in Dorian's mind. Could that be what was holding Raif back? She didn't care if he was penniless, but men had their pride. Especially Raif. He'd be even more sensitive because she was so successful. Silly man, Dorian thought fondly. If that was his only problem, she was in a position to solve it.

Raif and Dorian left soon after that, with no protests from Carrie or Barnaby.

As Raif walked her to her car, Dorian said, "They'll be so good for each other."

"Yes, I like happy endings," he said. She refrained from saying the obvious as he opened the driver's side door and told her, "I'll follow you to my house."

"I can't stay tonight, Raif," she answered regretfully. "The real estate agent called early this morning. If he phones again tomorrow morning, I really should be home to take the call."

"Okay, I'll meet you at your house. I'll put my truck in your garage. It's such a simple solution. I don't know why I didn't think of it before."

"I'm just as glad you didn't. I enjoyed being a house-guest." She smiled.

"Not nearly as much as I enjoyed having you." He leaned down and kissed the tip of her nose. "Come on, I'll race you home."

When they reached her house, Dorian asked, "Would you like coffee?"

"No, I want *you*." Raif took her in his arms.

"You don't waste any time, do you?" She laughed.

His face sobered. "I need to make the most of the time I have."

That gave her a perfect opportunity to discuss his future...and theirs. But when Raif's hands slid under her T-shirt to caress her bare skin, Dorian decided the present was more important.

"You're wearing a bra," he said disapprovingly.

"You have a degree in engineering. Can't you do something about that?" she teased.

"Believe it!" He stripped off her shirt and unfastened her bra.

A current of electricity raced through her as he stroked her breasts slowly, gazing at them with glowing eyes. His fingertips tantalized her, circling her nipples without touching them.

"Let's go upstairs," she whispered.

"I don't want to let go of you that long."

Raif's hands glided down to span her slender waist, holding her while his mouth moved sensuously over hers. As she parted her lips in invitation, he unsnapped her jeans and slid his hands inside to cup her bottom. But when she tried to close the small space between them, his hands moved around to caress her thighs.

Dorian's entire body responded to his sensual fondling. The sweet torment turned to an insistent demand as he explored her secret, sensitive places.

"You're driving me wild," she gasped.

"I love to touch you," he murmured. "Your body is like warm silk."

His seductive probing was almost more than she could bear. Dorian threw her arms around Raif's neck and forced their bodies together. He shuddered in response, and kissed her deeply.

With his mouth possessing hers, she unbuttoned his shirt and raked her nails restlessly through the crisp hair on his chest, tracing the tapering V to his waist. After unbuckling his obstructing belt, she slid his zipper down. As his slacks fell to the floor, she urged his shorts over his hips.

"Now you're driving *me* crazy," he muttered.

"I love to touch you, too."

Raif's long body went rigid when she caressed him intimately. He crushed her in his arms, making her burningly aware of his boundless need. Raif's frantic kiss was further proof of his unbridled passion. His tongue plunged again and again in a symbolic mating.

He kicked off his hampering clothes and removed the remainder of Dorian's. Their nude bodies now conformed in a scorching contact that welded them together.

"You're part of me," Raif groaned. "How can I give you up?"

"I won't let you!"

Dorian tightened her hold around his neck so convulsively that he lost his balance and sank to the bottom step of the staircase, carrying her with him. He pulled her onto his lap, clutching her close with one arm around her shoulders and the other under her knees.

She framed his face between her palms. "Love me, darling."

"Like never before," he promised.

Dorian was asking for more than the physical act, but when Raif turned her to face him, conscious thought ceased. Pure sensation took over. His throbbing masculinity teased her nerve endings, setting her on fire. She gripped his hips with her knees as Raif fueled the flames with his driving power. The storm he created built in intensity, pounding their bodies with wave after wave of spiraling sensation. A final burst brought complete fulfillment. Taut muscles relaxed as the intensity of their passion diminished to a shared contentment.

"That *was* like never before," Raif murmured when his breathing slowed.

"It always is," Dorian answered blissfully.

"That's true." He shifted her on his lap and hugged her knees against his body. "Each time with you is special."

Raif was stroking her hair so tenderly that Dorian knew this was the time to bring up the future. He certainly couldn't deny his feelings for her. First, though, she had to remove his self-imposed obstacles.

"We have to talk, Raif."

She thought his body tensed, but evidently not. He nibbled on her ear teasingly. "You sound so serious. Any complaints?"

"Have I ever had?"

"That's one way I've never failed you, anyway." When she lifted her head to look at him uncertainly, his set expression changed to a smile. "But what man wouldn't want to make love to you every chance he got?"

Dorian wasn't fooled. Raif was still scarred by the past, yet it would be so different in the future. She had to convince him of that.

"There are some things I'd like to explain," she began.

He arched his back and winced. "Would you mind if I stood up, honey? The edge of the step is digging into my back."

She scrambled off his lap and held out her hand to help him up. "You poor thing. Why didn't you say something sooner?"

"I didn't notice it until just now." He smiled. "I wonder why?"

"I wouldn't have a clue," she answered demurely.

"Let's go upstairs and get comfortable."

Dorian laughed, gesturing at their nude bodies. "How much more comfortable can we get?"

"Let's work on it." He took her hand and led her up the stairs.

When they were in bed, Dorian snuggled happily into Raif's arms. Even after the sexual tension was eased, she loved the feeling of their legs twined together and his warm, supple body pressing against hers.

"I'd like to stay here like this forever." She sighed rapturously.

"You'd have to get up for meals," he teased. "Living on love is merely an expression."

"I never thought *you'd* turn practical."

His arms loosened slightly. "You're calling me a grass-hopper again."

"Not critically," she said hastily. "Enjoying the moment is a charming quality."

"But?" he asked evenly.

Dorian picked her way carefully. "You used to want to try so many things."

"I've tried most of them."

"You can't give up because everything didn't turn out the way you expected," she said earnestly.

He moved away to lie on his back with his arms crossed under his head. "I'll admit I have regrets about some of the things I've done. Everyone does."

"That doesn't mean the next thing you try will be a failure."

He turned his head to stare at her searchingly. "That's the ultimate disgrace in your eyes, isn't it, Dorian? To be a failure."

"No!"

She ached to tell him she didn't care if he dug ditches for a living, as long as that made him happy. But little indications told her Raif *wasn't* happy. How could she convince him that she only wanted to help?

"Everyone's god isn't money," he said.

"You think mine is?" she asked quietly.

"I think your consciousness could stand raising, but you're not alone there. Be happy with your success, Dorian. You deserve it."

"I could help you fulfill *your* ambitions, too, Raif. Tell me what kind of job you want, and I'll find it for you."

"I didn't fulfill your expectations before. Why don't you just give up on me?"

"Don't you know why?" she asked sadly.

Raif got out of bed and went to stand by the window. In the moonlight streaming in, his nude body was perfectly sculpted. "We've just shared a very beautiful experience," he said. "You're trying to convince yourself that's all that matters, but we both know it isn't."

In spite of all her efforts, she'd wounded his pride. Raif was withdrawing from her again.

"I wasn't suggesting you couldn't succeed on your own," she said in a small voice. "I know you don't need me."

He turned away from the window. She couldn't see his expression because the light was at his back. But when he answered her, his voice was tender.

"Is that what you think?" He sat on the edge of the bed and reached out to stroke her cheek.

"I don't know what to think," she replied hopelessly.

"Then don't try." He took her in his arms and trailed his lips over her shoulder. "We're together here and now. That's what counts."

"What about tomorrow?" she asked hesitantly.

"We'll be together then, too."

She meant *tomorrow* in the larger sense. Did Raif? Dorian was unwilling to ask, afraid of hearing the answer. Maybe he was right about living for the moment. What could be more perfect than this one?

When Raif urged her gently backward onto the pillows Dorian held out her arms to him.

Chapter Nine

Dorian and Raif were still asleep the next morning when the telephone rang. He scowled and buried his head under the pillow as she fumbled around blindly.

"I hope I didn't get you out of the shower," John Saputo said.

"No, I...wasn't doing anything important." She smiled at the long mound in the bed next to her.

"Just sleeping," Raif muttered in a muffled voice.

"I have good news for you," the agent said. "The Bronwyns made an offer on your house."

"That's nice," Dorian answered tepidly. "How much?"

"Well, it isn't quite what you're asking, but the market is very depressed right now. Nothing is moving. I really think we were lucky to get any kind of an offer this fast."

"How much?" she repeated evenly, becoming more wide awake. When he named an amount, she sat up straight. "For this house? You must be joking!"

"Well, now, you have to consider—"

She cut him off sharply. "They must think I'm simple-minded to make an offer like that."

"I might be able to get them up a little," he said cautiously.

"They'd have to come up a *lot* to even be in the ballpark!"

"I'm not sure how high they'll go. They liked the house, but there are a lot of properties on the market right now."

"Then I suggest they look at them. Call me again when you have a buyer who lives in the real world." She banged the receiver down furiously.

Raif peeked out from under the pillow. "I gather a celebration isn't in order."

"I knew I didn't like those Bronwyns," she said balefully. "You wouldn't believe what they offered."

"This is just the opening round. Most people put in a low bid, figuring they can always come up. The realtor will go back and tell them it was refused, and then you'll negotiate."

"I hate to haggle, especially with them. They're the kind of people who aren't satisfied until they have the gold fillings out of your teeth."

"You don't have to worry." Raif poked a finger in her mouth playfully. "Your teeth are perfect—like the rest of you." When she bit his finger he yelped. "Don't take it out on me."

She smiled, her good humor returning. "I can't bite the Bronwyns. I might get rabies."

They were having breakfast when the phone rang again. Dorian's jaw set grimly, but this time it was Carrie.

After they'd discussed the exciting developments of the previous night, Carrie asked, "Would you happen to know where Raif is? I called early this morning, but he wasn't home."

"He's sitting right here. He...uh...he came over early to help me clean out the basement." Dorian avoided Raif's amused gaze.

"What a good friend," Carrie remarked innocently.

"Yes." Dorian's voice softened. "I don't know what I'd do without Raif. Do you want to talk to him?"

"I was hoping he'd come over and hook up the VCR for us. It was delivered with a lot of other equipment this morning. But I don't want to take him away if he's helping you."

"You're a wonder, Carrie. I should think after last night you'd have more pressing things on your mind."

"I do. That's why I want to get the youth program set up and functioning as soon as possible. So I can go on my honeymoon."

"Did you and Barnaby set the date after we left?"

"Not precisely, but Barnaby wants it to be soon. I do, too." Carrie laughed like a young girl.

"I'd feel the same way," Dorian said wistfully. "Have you decided where you're going on your honeymoon?"

"I'll tell you all about it when I see you. Right now I'm knee-deep in cartons that need unpacking."

"I'm sure Raif will be happy to help."

"What are you volunteering me for?" he asked.

"Something about a VCR. Carrie is trying to whip the Center into shape. She could use you there this morning."

"Do you have any plans for us today?"

"I hadn't thought about it. You won't be there all day, will you?"

"A couple of hours should do it," he assured her. "Tell Carrie I'll be there as soon as I finish breakfast." When Dorian had relayed the message and hung up he said,

"While I'm gone you can think of something you'd like to do today." He laughed as her fair skin turned rosy. "In addition to that."

Carrie looked harassed when Raif reached the Center. The usually neat room was littered with wrapping paper and sections of cardboard, and she was frowning at the booklet in her hand.

"What's the problem?" he asked.

"I've been trying to find out how to work this thing, but the instructions are written in Sanskrit."

"Not to worry," he soothed. "Little kids can do it."

"They can also turn cartwheels and stand on their heads. That doesn't mean *I'll* ever be able to."

"This is simpler. Trust me."

She raised an eyebrow in skepticism. "Okay, what does this mean? 'Attach one end of the five-foot 300-OHM twin-lead connector cable to the UHF OUT terminals.'"

"Nothing you have to be concerned with. That's my department. After I get it hooked up I'll show you how it operates, and you'll be as smart as any little kid."

Raif completed the job rapidly. After simplifying the instructions for Carrie, he asked what else needed to be done.

"I hate to impose. Dorian is probably expecting you back," she said tentatively.

He didn't satisfy her curiosity. "As long as I'm here, I might as well finish up. What's next?"

"You're going to think I'm hopelessly incompetent, but I can't figure out how to put up the badminton net."

"That's easy. Just be sure it's stretched tightly so it doesn't sag in the middle."

"But what do I tie it to?"

"I'll get some concrete and sink two poles in the ground."

"That sounds like a big job."

"Not really. After I stop by my place for a post digger, I'll pick up a couple of uprights and a bag of cement."

"I'll pay for everything of course, and this time I intend to pay for your labor, too."

Raif looked at her in amusement. "Why is this time any different?"

"We're not operating on a shoestring anymore. I have Barnaby's lovely check."

"Keep it. You'll be surprised at how fast it disappears."

"No, Raif. You've been very generous, but you know that old saying—rich or poor, it's nice to have money."

"I manage to get by," he answered dryly.

"I didn't mean to hurt your feelings," she said uncertainly.

"You will if you don't drop the subject."

"Oh, dear. I should have listened to Barnaby."

"You discussed my financial situation with him?"

Carrie was startled at the hard note in Raif's voice. "I wouldn't call it a discussion. I simply said I'd taken advantage of you long enough. That from now on you deserve to be paid for the work you do."

"What did he say?"

"He said you offered out of friendship, and I should accept graciously."

Raif's set jaw relaxed. "I knew I was right about Barnaby."

"I never thought I'd meet a man like him," Carrie answered rapturously.

After Raif returned with the necessary equipment, Carrie kept him company while he dug two holes in the ground and set a couple of poles in cement. It was hot work under the direct sun, and he soon took off his shirt.

Carrie admired the muscles that rippled over his bronze torso. "Hard labor certainly keeps a man fit. You and Barnaby are both so nice and trim."

Raif paused to straighten up and give her a white-toothed grin. "You'd know more about his fitness than I would."

"It isn't nice to tease an old lady." She laughed.

"Not you, Carrie," he answered fondly. "You're still young enough for romance, aren't you?"

"I never expected to fall in love again," she said softly. "My first marriage was so good. I can't believe I'm being given a second chance at happiness."

"They say people who were happily married are the ones who marry again." Raif turned away and went back to work.

Carrie watched the controlled ferocity in his movements. "When are you going to stop letting pride ruin your life?" she asked quietly.

"Leave it alone, Carrie," he warned.

"I wouldn't be a good friend if I did. I saw you and Dorian together last night. You can't tell me it's over between you."

"It won't ever be over. I found that out, unfortunately. But time and distance help. When I don't see her, the pain eases after a while. Only a fool would keep jabbing himself in the heart."

"But you *are* seeing her. You were at her house this morning."

"And I will be again tomorrow. God knows we both tried not to get involved, but I suppose it was inevitable.

After she leaves here, though, I never expect to see her again,'' Raif said in a dead voice.

"Does she knew that?" Carrie asked incredulously.

"It's for her own good as much as mine," he answered indirectly.

"What if she doesn't agree with you?"

"She will when she goes back to her normal life. Dorian isn't thinking clearly now. She only wants to remember how good it was."

"What's wrong with that?"

"Marriage is more than romance. There has to be trust. Merely sharing her bed isn't good enough for me," he said flatly.

"Raif, if you'd only—"

"The subject is closed, Carrie."

His grim face warned her not to pursue it. After an uncomfortable moment, she asked, "How long should I wait before I attach the net to those things?"

"They'll set up overnight." Raif forced a smile. "I'll expect a call tomorrow morning telling me the net is all knotted."

"That's a male chauvinist remark," she said with mock indignation. "I'm not totally incompetent."

They tried to joke as they usually did, but the easy camaraderie was missing. Raif left a short time later.

Dorian was doing the breakfast dishes when her secretary telephoned that morning.

"You must have a lot of confidence in me," Karen said. "I thought you'd be on the phone regularly."

"I knew you could handle anything that came up." Dorian sounded serene, but she was a little shocked to realize she hadn't given her office a thought in days.

"I appreciate the compliment, but I don't mind admitting I'll be glad when you're back."

Dorian frowned. "Is anything wrong?"

"Just the usual office politics. Graybar says Lowell takes all the plush jobs for his own clients."

Dorian relaxed. "You should be used to that by now."

"I suppose so, but their secretaries are starting to bicker, too. I'll be glad when Friday gets here."

"Everybody looks forward to Friday. If they give you any real trouble, call me."

"I'll manage for two more days. Then they're your babies."

"What do you mean?" Dorian asked in alarm. "Where are you going?"

"Nowhere. I was referring to the cocktail party. You'll be back for that."

"It's *this* Friday night?"

"Don't tell me you forgot? It's a good thing I called."

"But that's only two days away. I can't leave that soon!"

"You're kidding me, aren't you? You *have* to be here. You're the hostess."

"I guess you're right." Dorian sighed.

"I don't understand you." Karen sounded baffled. "You were all fired up about this party before you left."

"I still am." Dorian tried to sound convincing. "I just hate to leave things unfinished here." *That* was the absolute truth.

"How much more can you have to do?"

"There are all kinds of loose ends," Dorian answered vaguely. "Plus the fact that the house isn't sold yet."

"Surely you don't intend to stay there until it is? Houses sometimes remain on the market for months."

"I'm finding that out."

"What do you plan to do? It's one heck of a long commute."

"I couldn't do that, obviously. But I might have to spend weekends here."

"That's a real bummer," Karen said.

Dorian's soft mouth curved in a smile. "Yeah, it's a dirty job, but somebody's got to do it."

"Well, at least you have the party to look forward to. I talked to the florist, and I've been on the phone to Corso daily. You can count on it being a smash bash."

"You're a wonder worker, Karen. I won't forget what you've done," Dorian said gratefully.

Her smile faded as she hung up the receiver. She didn't want to leave Raif now. Not when every night brought them closer together. He was fighting against it, but given time, he'd come to realize they belonged to each other.

That was the whole problem. She didn't have unlimited time. Raif was weakening now, she was sure of it. But if she left him, even briefly, he'd start having second thoughts. The magic only worked when they were together.

Suddenly Dorian's face lit up. She'd invite Raif to come with her! It would be like a second honeymoon. They'd go to museums and the theater, and eat in wonderful restaurants. The expense gave her a moment's pause. Raif couldn't afford to take her those places, and his pride wouldn't allow her to pay. The problem wasn't insurmountable, however. She could say the tickets were repayment for favors, and the dinners were some other kind of perk. This might be just what Raif needed to give him that extra push, a really romantic interlude.

She was fizzing with excitement when the telephone rang a second time. This call didn't delight her. It was the real estate agent again.

"I spoke to the Bronwyns," he announced. "I told them you rejected their offer, and they're prepared to raise it."

"How much?" When he told her, Dorian said flatly, "That's not enough."

"Well, I wouldn't be too hasty, Miss Merrill."

"The house is worth more. We all know it."

"That may be true, but you have to be flexible. You come down a little, and maybe they'll come up a little more."

"Wouldn't it make better sense if they gave you their top price, and I'll tell you if it's acceptable?"

He chuckled indulgently. "The real estate business isn't conducted that way."

"It would save a lot of phone calls," she remarked, stifling her annoyance.

"That's all part of the job. So... how much are you willing to come down?"

"I'll have to think about it," she answered coolly.

"You don't want to wait around. The whole deal might fall through if you play hardball," he warned. "Buyers are tricky. You have to get their signature on a contract before they have second thoughts."

"I guess I'll just have to take that chance. I need to give the matter some thought."

He argued doggedly, but Dorian refused to be pinned down. She finally got rid of him and dismissed the whole matter from her mind. She had more important things to think about.

Dorian waited impatiently for Raif to come back, but he didn't return until late afternoon. She couldn't understand it, since he'd specifically told her to make plans for the day. And when she'd phoned the Center at noon, Carrie told her Raif had already left.

"Did he say where he was going?" Dorian asked.

"No."

"That's strange. We were supposed to do something today."

"I'm sorry," Carrie said in a muted voice.

"Is anything wrong?" Dorian asked uncertainly. "You sound funny. Everything's all right between you and Barnaby, isn't it?"

"Blissful, you might say." Carrie's voice warmed. "Can you believe he wants to take me to Los Angeles to pick out an engagement ring?"

"Accept," Dorian said promptly. "When are you planning to go? I have to go there on Friday for a business affair. If you're there, too, maybe the four of us can do the town over the weekend."

"The four of us?"

"I'm going to ask Raif to come with me."

There was a silence at the other end of the phone, then Carrie said, "I'll speak to Barnaby and get back to you."

"Do I detect a lack of enthusiasm?" Dorian laughed. "Okay, I can take a hint. You two want to be alone. But if I can do anything for you while you're in L.A., don't hesitate to call me."

"I hope you'll do the same if you ever need a friend," Carrie answered quietly.

Dorian was slightly puzzled after she hung up. Then she decided the older woman was just being sentimental. She *was* responsible for bringing Carrie and Barnaby together.

By the time Raif drove into the driveway, Dorian was slightly annoyed. "Where have you been?" she demanded.

"You know where I've been. I was at the Center helping Carrie."

"That was hours ago. I called there, and she said you left before noon."

"Were you checking up on me?" Raif asked evenly.

Dorian was taken aback by his cool tone. "No, of course not," she faltered. "I was getting a little worried, that's all. You said we'd go someplace today."

His jaw relaxed. "I'm sorry, honey. It was thoughtless of me to forget."

"It's all right. I didn't have anything special in mind. Did you get Carrie squared away?"

"Pretty much. I hooked up the VCR and dug some post holes. It was hot, sweaty work, so I went home and took a shower."

"You could have showered here." When he looked at her without expression, she added hastily, "But then you wouldn't have had clean clothes."

"Exactly." He smiled in a determined way. "Have you decided what you'd like to do?"

Dorian tried to mask her bewilderment. What had happened at the Center? Raif had left the house in a cheerful mood, and returned looking like a man with an insurmountable problem. Had he been wrestling with demons all afternoon? She ached to help, but whatever was on Raif's mind, he obviously wasn't ready to share it with her.

"Is it that hard to make a decision? There aren't that many places to go in Summerville," he said with forced humor.

"The afternoon is almost over," she answered absently, then realized that sounded like a complaint. "I mean, you're right. There isn't much to do here," she said quickly.

"I have an idea. Why don't we drive to Larkin and take in an early movie? We can have dinner there afterward."

"That's a great idea. I haven't seen a movie in ages. I'll go upstairs and change."

"Larkin isn't exactly a big city," he commented dryly. "You can go the way you are."

"I'm tired of pants. I bought a new outfit the other day and I want to wear it."

He shrugged. "Whatever you like." Raif didn't follow her upstairs.

Dorian changed into a slim beige skirt and a matching silk sweater that outlined her curves, hoping Raif would approve. He was so strangely remote. Her earlier delight over a romantic idyll in Los Angeles was dampened. This was no time to bring it up. Or was it? Perhaps that was just the thing to lift Raif's spirits. Dorian was filled with renewed enthusiasm as she went downstairs.

"How do I look?" She twirled around for his inspection.

"Very nice." He held out his hand for her car keys. "I'll drive."

Dorian had always driven when they took her car. She didn't mind letting him take over, but the implication bothered her. Raif was indicating a need to be in control. What was making him feel so helpless?

Since she didn't know what subjects to avoid, and Raif was preoccupied, conversation between them was stilted. Finally Dorian gave up entirely and stared out the window at the passing orange groves.

When they were halfway to Larkin, Raif slanted a glance at her. "You're very quiet. Are you still angry at me for standing you up this afternoon?"

"I was never angry. I just missed you."

He reached over and squeezed her hand. "You're very sweet."

Dorian was encouraged enough to ask tentatively, "Is everything all right, Raif?"

"Couldn't be better. I'm sorry I came back in such a foul mood, honey. I'll make it up to you, I promise."

"You don't have to apologize. Everyone's entitled to feel out of sorts now and then."

"But not to take it out on another person."

"Sometimes it helps to talk about what's bothering you," she remarked casually.

"I can handle it." As if realizing he wasn't giving that impression, Raif said soberly. "When something can't be changed, you learn to live with the fact. But once in a while I find that hard to accept."

Since she could tell he didn't intend to confide in her, Dorian switched tactics. "Maybe you simply need a change of scenery. I have to return to Los Angeles on Friday for that corporate cocktail party you heard me planning. Why don't you come with me? We could—"

"No!" He cut her off sharply.

Dorian discovered too late that her timing was faulty, but she persevered. "At least you could think about it. You don't have to make up your mind this minute."

"I don't want to think about it." A muscle in his jaw twitched.

"You're being stubborn, Raif. We could have a wonderful time, and it would do you good to get away."

"From what?" he asked harshly.

Dorian bit her lip. She'd hurt his feelings again by calling attention to the difference in their situations. She was returning on business; he'd be going along because he had no job to keep him here. How could she repair the damage?

Raif didn't give her a chance. "Forget it, Dorian. I don't want to discuss it any further."

The atmosphere was more strained between them than before. She didn't know what to do about it, and he didn't seem to care. Although Raif was the one who finally broke the silence.

"What did you do all day?" he asked.

"I'm afraid I was shamelessly lazy."

"It's always nice to have a day like that."

Dorian was afraid another lull would fall so she rushed on. "I washed my hair and talked to Sally for quite a while. They cut Ken's hours again. She didn't come out and say so, but I think they're having trouble making ends meet."

"That's too bad. Ken is a good man."

"Sally hates the idea of moving away from Summerville, but Ken says they might have to."

"I doubt if it will come to that. Tell her to think positively."

"That doesn't pay the rent." Dorian sighed. "Oh, that reminds me. John Saputo phoned today. The Bronwyns upped their offer." She told him the new one. "Saputo was wrong. It does pay to play hardball."

"Up to a point. You can't play *too* hard to get or they'll lose interest."

"You sound like John. I'm inclined to take my chances."

"I wouldn't advise it, Dorian. It's not a bad offer when you look at the bottom line. As long as your house stays on the market, you're paying taxes, insurance and upkeep. Once you sell it, you not only save those expenses, you have a lump sum of money to invest that will earn interest. You're actually getting your selling price when you balance the debits and credits."

"You sound like one of those economists in the newspaper," Dorian said. "How do you know so much about finance?"

His smile held irony. "I read a lot of newspapers. Anyway, you should give it some consideration before you reject the Bronwyns' offer."

Dorian didn't want to mention the real reason for her reluctance, and it didn't seem to have occurred to Raif that she wouldn't be around once the house was sold. Or had he accepted the fact?

"I'll think about it," she murmured.

They bought a newspaper when they reached Larkin and chose a funny movie. Raif suggested a love story that claimed to have gotten rave reviews, but Dorian was afraid it would only depress her. They both needed cheering up.

The comedy was a wise selection. Their tension eased as they ate popcorn and chuckled at the antics on the big screen. None of the problems in the film were earth shattering, and all were resolved by the end of the movie.

"That was a good choice," Raif remarked as they got into the car afterward. He was still smiling. "Where would you like to go for dinner?"

"I'm surprised you're hungry after all the popcorn you ate."

"We had one little box for the two of us," he said dismissively.

"It was a big box, and you ate most of it."

"I offered to buy you your own."

"I like to share." She smiled.

He leaned over and kissed her. "I do, too, as long as it's with you."

Dorian glowed with happiness. Raif was his old self again. She worried too much about these little setbacks.

Raif was a very complex man. But that only made him more fascinating.

The restaurant they chose had a strolling violinist. He wasn't a very good musician, but what he lacked in skill, he made up for in enthusiasm. The man lingered at their table, probably because of the generous tip Raif gave him, but Dorian was charmed. Her eyes met Raif's in a gaze full of mutual tenderness.

They had a leisurely dinner, savoring both food and atmosphere, as well as the anticipation of what would come later. When they were in the car driving back to Summerville, their sensibilities heightened.

Raif caressed Dorian's knee briefly. "The man who invented bucket seats should be strung up by some painful part of his anatomy," he grumbled.

"What don't you like about them?" Dorian knew perfectly well, but she wanted to hear him tell her.

"I want you close enough to touch."

"You're too old to make out in a car."

He turned his head to give her a glance that made her elbows tingle. "Would you like me to prove you're wrong?"

She laughed breathlessly. "Don't tempt me."

His answering chuckle was wholly male. "I plan to do more than that when we get home."

Raif kept his promise. They made love in Dorian's bed with the moonlight gleaming on their naked bodies. Tender, passionate love that satisfied their hunger until they awakened again with renewed desire. The night was spent in a private world of ecstasy. Neither the past nor the future were important. Their joined bodies, pulsing with mutual satisfaction, were the only reality.

The magic remained when they awakened late the next morning. Remembered pleasure softened the hard planes of Raif's face as he kissed Dorian gently.

"This is the best part of the day," he murmured. "Waking up and finding you in my arms."

"For me, too," she whispered.

After a companionable silence, Raif said, "Let's do something different today. Something we haven't done before."

"That rules out indoor sports." She grinned.

"You're shameless. I'm beginning to think all you want is my body," he said lightly.

"There aren't many like yours around." Her fingers trailed over his flat stomach.

He grasped her hand before it could glide lower. "I won't be used, woman." When she winced at his iron grip, the pressure eased and he threw back the covers. "Come on, let's have breakfast. Somehow I worked up a huge appetite."

It was a wonderful day, although they didn't do anything special. After a late breakfast they wandered through a formerly rundown section of Summerville that had been transformed into an art colony.

Some of the previously seedy stores were now little galleries displaying sculpture and paintings by local artists. Others sold ceramics and a variety of handicrafts.

"A lot of these artists are very talented," Raif remarked as they paused to glance in a window.

"Look at that gold rose on a chain. Isn't it lovely?" Dorian asked.

"Let's go inside and take a look," Raif suggested.

The saleswoman took the beautifully crafted piece out of the window and pressed a hidden spring. "It's a locket," she explained as the rose opened like a clamshell.

"How unusual," Dorian exclaimed. "No one would ever guess."

"Do you like it?" Raif asked.

"I love it!"

"You've just made a sale," he told the saleswoman.

"Raif, no. It looks expensive," Dorian protested.

"And worth whatever it costs. You can put my picture inside so you'll always remember me."

Dorian was silent as he clasped the chain around her neck. The locket slipped down to nestle between her breasts. It felt as cold as her heart. Why would she need Raif's picture to remind her of him? Didn't he plan on being around? She gazed up at him, but he was smiling.

"Okay, next stop is Jellison's for an ice cream cone." He gave the saleswoman his credit card. "They still make them with chocolate sprinkles on top. Remember those?"

Gradually Dorian was reassured. Raif didn't act like a man who was hiding something. He was not only completely relaxed, he was satisfyingly affectionate. When he wasn't holding her hand, he had an arm around her shoulders.

They whiled away the day aimlessly, simply enjoying the pleasure of being together. Once during the afternoon, Dorian did suggest dropping in at the Center to see how Carrie was getting along, but Raif vetoed the idea.

"She'll have to struggle along on her own," he said firmly. "This is *our* day."

It occurred to Dorian that it was the last one they'd have for a while unless Raif changed his mind about coming to Los Angeles with her. Surely he must be wavering, at least. She was tempted to ask him again, then decided to wait for a more opportune time. Her mouth curved in a secret smile as she pictured that moment.

"You look like the cat that hastened the canary's demise," Raif commented. "What mischief are you plotting?"

"Nothing you'll object to. At least I hope not." She gazed at him through long lashes.

"When you look at me like that I couldn't deny you anything," he said deeply.

"That's what I'm counting on," she murmured.

They decided to have dinner at Raif's house instead of going out to eat. He insisted on doing all the cooking, declaring Dorian was a guest.

"I don't want to be a guest, I want to help. Can't I peel the carrots or something?" she asked.

"You don't peel carrots, you scrape them."

"Picky, picky," she complained.

"All great chefs are," he answered calmly.

"Are they also this modest about their abilities?"

"Cooking is the only talent I brag about."

"You're good at everything you do," she said softly.

He glanced around, then came over to kiss her. "Are you trying to make me ruin our dinner?"

"I was only stating a fact. Don't you like compliments?"

"I love them." His hand curled around her nape as he kissed her with growing warmth. Just then something began to sizzle loudly on the stove. "Damn," Raif muttered, straightening up.

He strode over and pulled the frying pan off the burner. "From now on there will be no more seducing the cook," he ordered.

"Never?"

"I don't want to be unreasonable. How about for the next hour?"

She pretended to think it over, then nodded. "I can live with that."

After dinner they took a walk through the quiet, tree-lined streets. That was one of the joys of a small town, Dorian reflected: the scent of flowers filled the air, not exhaust fumes.

When they returned home, neither felt like doing anything more than lying on the couch together, listening to soft music on the stereo. It was a soothing ending to a perfect day.

The telephone rang a little later, intruding on their tranquility. Raif rose reluctantly, promising to get rid of the caller swiftly. It was Barnaby, though, and he didn't like to cut him off.

"Barnaby wants to discuss something with me, honey," Raif said apologetically. "Do you mind?"

"Not at all." She smiled reassuringly. "Take your time."

Since the conversation was lengthy, Dorian decided to treat herself to a bubble bath. It was a luxury she seldom had time for, and this was a day for indulging every whim, both large and small.

She was almost disappointed. The contents of Raif's bathroom cabinets were Spartan. Shampoo and bar soap were all he used. But tucked away in a corner, Dorian found a jar of scented bath crystals left behind by his mother.

While the tub filled with iridescent bubbles, Dorian undressed and placed a bath towel on a nearby stool. Then she stepped into the tub and sank beneath the foam with a contented sigh.

Raif found her there a short time later. Desire smol
dered in his emerald eyes as he sat on the edge of the tub
and dipped his fingers in the water.

"You look like a mermaid." His burning gaze swept
over her glistening shoulders and the slope of her bare
breasts.

She gave him a siren smile. "Mermaids are scaly, and
they don't have legs."

His hand slipped between her thighs, following their
length as far as he could go. "You're right," he murmured, caressing her tantalizingly. "You're all woman, my
love."

She closed her eyes and arched into his hand, lifting her
body. Raif lowered his head and kissed the cherry nipples
that peeped seductively through the froth.

"Ah, Raif, darling," she sighed.

His eyes glittered with an almost pagan light as he stared
at her passion-filled face. "Do you know what it does to
me to see you react like this?"

He reached down and lifted her out of the tub with a
fevered urgency. Water cascaded down her body as Raif
bonded her to him with one arm around her shoulders and
the other circling her hips.

"Your clothes are getting soaked," she whispered.

"Then you'd better help me take them off." His smile
was sensuous as he guided her hand to his belt buckle.

Dorian's fingers fumbled in her haste to undress him.
When his final garment had been kicked aside, he took an
oversize bath towel and wrapped it around both of them.
Raif's hands moved over her back to dry her, but the heat
generated by their locked bodies was enough. They were
both breathing rapidly when he swung her into his arms
and carried her into the bedroom.

That night Dorian reached heights she'd never known existed. Raif was like a man inspired. He explored every way possible of bringing her joy. His lovemaking was almost desperate in its intensity. Dorian was completely spent when they were finally quiet in each other's arms.

"I don't see how it could ever be like this again," she said wonderingly.

"It can't be." Raif stroked her hair tenderly.

Dorian was too replete to hear the sadness in his voice. She laughed softly. "I'll bet it can. What are you doing tomorrow night?"

"You'll be in Los Angeles."

"You can be, too. The invitation still stands."

"Thanks, but the answer is no," he said evenly.

"Think what it would mean, Raif," she coaxed. "We could have three more glorious days like today. Or more, if you want to stay."

"There won't be any more days like today," he said flatly.

"I'll admit this one was awesome, but we can try to better our average," she teased.

"Go back to Los Angeles, Dorian," he said tautly. "You've made a satisfying life for yourself. Enjoy it."

"You could enjoy it with me," she said uncertainly.

"Forget about me." His voice was harsh.

"You don't mean that. You couldn't! Not after today...tonight."

"This day was a moment out of time. A lovely memory to blot out all the bad ones."

"I see." She did...finally. "You were giving me a going-away present."

"I wouldn't put it that way," he answered carefully. "It was for my sake as much as yours."

"I'm glad I wasn't a disappointment," she replied bitterly.

Raif sighed. "I don't want to quarrel with you, Dorian, not tonight of all nights. Just accept the fact that we're wrong for each other."

How could he say that after the moving experiences they'd shared? Not only tonight, but ever since they'd been reunited. But Raif didn't consider sex enough to justify a lifetime together. If that was all it was for him, she had to agree.

"I guess you're right," she answered as soon as she could control her emotions. "I have a tendency to romanticize. We had fun together, but it's time to get real."

"I'm glad you agree."

"I do, now that you've put everything in perspective. It only makes good sense to end on a high note." Dorian was drowning in misery. She had to get away before she broke down and disgraced herself.

"Where are you going?" Raif asked as she got out of bed.

"I have to go home. I . . . uh . . . I have to pack."

"You can do that in the morning."

"No, I want to get an early start." She reached for her clothes.

Raif got out of bed and stood over her. "Are you sure I can't persuade you to stay?"

"A considerate guest knows when the party is over," she answered brightly.

"Dorian, dear," he said gently, trying to turn her to face him.

She pulled away. "It's lucky I have my car here. You don't have to take me home."

"I can't let you go like this." He cupped her cheek in his palm, then looked at her searchingly. "Are you crying?"

"Of course not!" She jerked free and scrubbed her cheeks with the back of her clenched fist.

"Look at me, Dorian."

"I have an allergy," she said, averting her face. "It acts up at inconvenient times, but it's nothing to worry about."

"I didn't mean to be cruel, sweetheart," he said, ignoring her lame excuse. "It's for your good more than mine. I want you to be happy."

"I know that." Tears poured down her face, now that subterfuge was useless.

"I'm not the man for you," he groaned, pulling her into his arms.

"I know," Dorian repeated, but she couldn't help running her hands over his nude body one last time.

He flinched, which brought them closer together. "If I went to Los Angeles with you, it wouldn't change anything."

"I won't ask you to do anything you don't want to do," she murmured.

"There isn't anything I *don't* want to do with you," he muttered as he carried her back to bed.

Much later, when Raif was asleep with his head on her breast, Dorian gazed at him with tremulous happiness. Raif might have doubts about the promise he'd finally given, but she didn't. The coming weekend would prove to him that they belonged together.

Chapter Ten ·

Dorian was afraid Raif might change his mind the next morning, but he was grimly resigned. She wished he was happier about his decision to go to Los Angeles with her, yet she was confident he would be once they arrived.

His mood that morning was difficult, to say the least. An argument was narrowly averted when Dorian was advising him about what clothes he'd need. She made the mistake of saying they could go shopping in L.A. for anything he was lacking.

"I do own more than jeans and T-shirts," he said curtly. "I'm not completely destitute."

"I never thought you were," she soothed.

"Then why did you assume I don't have a decent suit to wear?"

"It would be perfectly understandable if your wardrobe was...sketchy," she explained carefully. "There isn't much occasion for dressing up in Summerville, and you said you'd knocked around the world prior to coming home."

"I never really told you much about my life," he said slowly. "Maybe that was a mistake."

Dorian sneaked a peek at her watch. She didn't want to irritate Raif further by cutting him off, but she was anxious to get going.

He noticed her surreptitious glance. "Oh well, it's too late to worry about it now."

"We'll have lots of time to talk in the car," she promised.

When they were finally on their way, Raif seemed resigned to the fact. And when they reached Los Angeles, he started to show interest.

Dorian's condominium was in a highrise building on Sunset Boulevard. The gleaming white tower had blue awnings and a massive front door of spotless plate glass. A uniformed doorman came out to the car when Dorian drove up.

"Welcome back, Miss Merrill," he said warmly. "You've been gone a long time."

"It does seem that way, Henry," she answered. "It's good to be home. There are some suitcases in the trunk."

"I'll bring them right up," he promised.

Raif looked around the plush lobby appraisingly. "You've done well for yourself," he commented.

"Wait till you see the view from my apartment."

Dorian led Raif through the large rooms, opening all the windows to get rid of the stuffiness. At the end of the tour of inspection, she led him onto a terrace that overlooked the city.

"Very impressive," he said approvingly.

"It's breathtaking at night. I love to lie in bed and stare out at the lights in the distance."

Raif smiled. "You won't mind if I focus my attention a little closer to home?"

"I wouldn't have it any other way." She flung her arms around his neck. "Oh, Raif, I'm so glad you're here!"

"I am, too," he answered, sounding slightly surprised.

Dorian drew back reluctantly. "I hate to leave you, but I have to go to the office. Karen must need help with all the last-minute details of the cocktail party."

"I'll go with you."

"Wouldn't you rather unpack and simply relax? It's going to be a long night."

"Are you ashamed to let your colleagues see your country boyfriend?" Raif's joking tone didn't compensate for the hardness of his eyes.

"Why do you say things like that when you know they're not true?" Dorian decided the time had come to bring the issue out into the open. "Does my success make you feel inadequate, Raif? It shouldn't. You can do anything you set your mind to. You've demonstrated that. I never would have asked you to come here if I thought your pride would suffer."

"I'm sorry, darling." He pulled her back into his arms. "Why can't I just let myself be happy?"

"I'll teach you how." Dorian stroked his hair gently. "The first lesson starts tonight."

"I'm not busy at the moment." He worried her earlobe delicately with his teeth.

"Unfortunately I am." She sighed.

"Boy, you're sure a different woman in the big city."

She looked at him swiftly, but Raif seemed genuinely amused. "Wait till you see how I crack the whip around the office," she answered lightly.

"I can hardly wait. Let's go, boss."

"I have to change clothes first."

After practically living in jeans, Dorian felt strange in high heels and a plain, navy linen suit. Raif was even more of a shock when he came out of the guest room. He'd hung his clothes in there after a look at Dorian's crowded closet.

"You look fantastic!" she exclaimed.

He was wearing a lightweight tweed jacket over gray slacks and a crisp, white shirt. Dorian was knowledgeable enough about men's clothes to know the jacket had been custom tailored. The draping was perfect, and the fabric expensive, evidence of Raif's former affluence.

"I'd be more flattered if you didn't sound so surprised," he said dryly.

"Well, you must admit it's a change from bare skin," she said impishly.

"Which do you prefer?" He grinned.

"If I told you, we wouldn't get to the office, and my assistant might quit."

Raif's handsome face and impressive physique drew many admiring glances from the women in Dorian's office. Her secretary was especially intrigued.

"What profession are you in, Mr. Dangerfield?" Karen asked after Dorian had introduced them.

"I'm between jobs at the moment," he answered.

"That's why our clients come to us, but I'm sure we'll be able to place you without any trouble." Her eyes moved over Raif's broad shoulders approvingly.

He chuckled. "Don't you want to know what I do?"

"I'm sure you're good at whatever it is," she murmured.

Dorian glanced up from the papers she was scanning, and remarked absently, "Raif isn't a client."

"I'm sorry," Karen apologized as Dorian went into her office.

"It was a natural mistake." He took pity on her obvious curiosity. "Dorian and I are old friends from Summerville."

"That explains a lot." Karen nodded in sudden understanding.

Dorian came out of her office carrying a sheet of paper. "I don't see Steven Kellerman's name on the list," she told Karen. "Are you sure he got his invitation?"

"I contacted him to double-check," Karen answered. "I didn't include him in the count because he might have to fly out early. But if he does show up, one more won't make any difference."

"I can see you're busy," Raif remarked. "I'll get out of your hair."

"You don't have to go. Karen can get you some magazines from the waiting room, and you can read them in my office," Dorian answered.

"You don't have to amuse me. I'm a big boy."

As her eyes followed Raif down the hall, Karen said, "That's the understatement of the year. Now I know why you forgot about the party. That man is enough to make a fish forget how to swim."

"He's pretty fantastic, isn't he?" Dorian asked softly.

"If you let him get away, you're brain dead."

"I don't intend to this time." Dorian returned to her office before Karen could ask questions.

Dorian was dragging her anchor when she returned to the apartment late in the day. Raif had changed to brief white shorts, and was sitting on the balcony with a drink in his hand, contemplating the view.

"You look beat," he commented as he joined her in the bedroom.

"I am." She kicked off her shoes and dropped her purse on the dressing table. "Everything piled up while I was gone. There were a million things that needed my attention."

"That's the price of owning your own company. Can I fix you a drink?"

"No thanks, it might put me to sleep. We only have an hour to dress and get to the restaurant."

"Take off your clothes and lie down. I'll relax you."

"I wish I could, but we don't have time."

He chuckled. "There are other ways to relax. I meant, I'll rub your back. If I had anything else in mind, I'd undress you myself."

Dorian stripped to her panties and bra and lay on her stomach. Raif straddled her legs and massaged her back with long soothing strokes. Her tense muscles gradually relaxed and her fatigue vanished.

"Mmm, that feels wonderful," she murmured.

"I thought it would."

"What did you do today?" she asked.

"Wandered around getting reacquainted with L.A. I haven't been here in a long time."

"What did you think of it?" She tensed slightly, waiting for his answer.

"It's a very exciting city. I like the feeling of energy."

Dorian's body relaxed. "I was sorry I couldn't be with you. I didn't even get a chance to show you around the office and introduce you to everybody."

"I met Walter Graybar as I was leaving. We struck up a conversation waiting for the elevator. He seems like a nice fellow."

"Yes, Walter is very pleasant," Dorian answered vaguely.

"Do I sense a slight reservation?" Raif asked.

"No, I was thinking of something else. I looked at the latest profit-and-loss sheet today, and the figures weren't what I expected." She turned over and sat up against the headboard. "I don't understand it, because we wrote even more business than I projected."

"Do you think your accountant is indulging in creative bookkeeping?"

"I'd hate to believe that. He's been with me for quite a while."

"That's no guarantee. I'll be happy to take a look at your books for you if you like."

"No thanks," she declined promptly. "You're here on vacation."

"I do know something about business."

"I'm sure you do," she answered in a soothing tone.

"You're sure of just the opposite." Raif sighed. "It's my fault for not being more open with you. We need to have a talk, Dorian."

She glanced at the clock. "Can it wait till later, darling? I want to be there in plenty of time, and we still have to get dressed."

Everything was running smoothly when Dorian and Raif arrived at the trendy restaurant. A bar was set up against one wall of the private room reserved for her cocktail party, and a buffet table stretched along another wall.

In the center of the table was a beautiful floral arrangement of red and white roses in a silver epergne. Platters of elaborate hors d'oeuvres covered the linen tablecloth, looking like miniature works of art.

"Now I know where the profits went," Raif commented as he gazed at caviar, smoked salmon and giant prawns.

"Every bite is an investment," Dorian answered.

"Wouldn't it be cheaper to hand out dollar bills?"

"Money doesn't taste this good." She took a toast point spread with paté and topped with a slice of truffle. "Mmm, you should try these. They're divine."

"I've been coveting one of those shrimp, but I was afraid you'd yell at me if I messed up the fancy arrangement." He indicated a perfect circle of pink prawns spread in a fan shape around a cup of remoulade sauce.

"You can have anything your little heart desires," she said fondly.

"I'll remind you of that later," he answered with a smile.

"You won't have to."

She gazed at him with frank admiration. Raif's dark suit was quietly elegant, and his snowy linen accentuated his deep tan. He would hold his own among the captains of industry she'd invited.

He lifted an eyebrow. "Do I have a smudge on my face? You're staring at me."

"I like to look at you," she replied honestly. "You're extremely handsome tonight."

"You're very sweet." His voice was warm with affection.

"Are you glad now that you came?"

"Very glad."

It wasn't just a polite response. Raif's voice rang with sincerity. Dorian was bubbling with happiness as she turned to greet the first arrivals.

That was the last chance she and Raif had for a private conversation. The room began to fill rapidly with well-dressed people.

Dorian moved among them with confidence. She smiled and made small talk with each group, while unobtrusively making sure everyone had a drink, and no one felt left out.

Raif would have been content to stand on the sidelines watching her admiringly, but Dorian kept him by her side. She introduced him to each group and told him what companies the various people represented, without mentioning Raif's occupation . . . or lack of it.

No one seemed to notice. Raif's genuine interest led them to talk about themselves. Inevitably, one of the guests, the president of an electronics firm, asked what field Raif was in.

"I'm an engineer," he answered.

"Structural or product engineering?"

"I spent my early career building bridges and dams, and then I moved into home construction."

"Good thinking. The liability factor on those big government projects is awesome. What's the name of your company?"

Raif hesitated for a split second before replying, "I'm in the process of forming a new one at the moment."

Before he was asked any more questions, Dorian made a polite excuse and led him away. In the few moments they were alone together, she said, "You could have told Carstairs the truth. You have nothing to be embarrassed about."

"I did, and I wasn't," Raif smiled.

Dorian wasn't fooled. "*I* know you've done important things in your life."

"You're the most important thing that's ever happened to me," he said fondly.

"I mean it, Raif. You don't have to put up a front for my sake. If any of these people think less of you because you aren't in their income bracket, they're not very perceptive."

"Don't let it bother you, honey," Raif soothed.

"I want you to have a good time," she said uncertainly.

"Stop worrying about me." He squeezed her hand. "Go back to your guests before I create a sensation by making passionate love to the hostess in front of everybody."

Raif went to the bar for a drink, where he chatted with the other people clustered there. He also visited the buffet table and talked with different guests. He was a good listener, so he never lacked for company. Dorian's worries were groundless. Raif was completely at ease in the scintillating company.

The evening eventually wound to a close, although the party was so successful that people were reluctant to leave. It was much later than Dorian had anticipated before the last guest departed.

"I thought we'd be out of here long ago," she apologized to Raif.

"That proves everybody had a good time."

"It did seem to go over well. Were you terribly bored, darling?"

"I had a ball. I haven't rubbed elbows with the moneyed classes in a long time." He grinned.

"Thank goodness it's over." She sighed. "You can tell the parking attendant to bring the car round. I have to talk to Corso for one minute, and then I'll join you out front."

In the car going home Raif asked, "Did you have anything to eat?"

"I was too busy."

"That's what I thought. We'll stop and get you something."

"I'm not really hungry. All I want to do is go home and take off my shoes."

"Okay, I'll make you some scrambled eggs."

"That's too much trouble. Unless you're hungry."

"You do have eggs in the refrigerator, don't you?"

"I'm not sure," she admitted.

Raif pulled into the parking lot of an all-night market. "I'll be right back," he promised.

By the time he returned with two large grocery bags, Dorian was half asleep. She struggled to suppress yawns all the way home.

When they reached the apartment, Raif sent her to get undressed, and Dorian didn't argue this time. She went into the bedroom and kicked off her high-heeled satin pumps with a sigh of relief. After changing to a chiffon and lace peignoir set in a delicate shade of peach, she returned to the kitchen.

The glass-topped table was set, and Raif was buttering a stack of toast. He glanced up and appraised her briefly. "Very nice," he commented.

"I wanted to show you I do own a nightgown." She smiled.

"It's beautiful, like you." He set a steaming plate of bacon and eggs in front of her. "Eat it while its hot," he instructed as he went back to the stove to fill his own plate.

Dorian took an appreciative bite of scrambled eggs. "This is a good idea. Now we won't have to waste time in the morning on breakfast."

"Are you going into the office?"

"No way! Tomorrow is Saturday."

"I thought you often worked on weekends."

"Only because I didn't have anything better to do." She gave him a melting smile. "Which doesn't apply to *this* weekend."

"What do you have planned for us?"

"I'll leave that up to you."

"One thing I'd like to do is take a ride around the city, especially the downtown area. I hear it's been extensively revitalized."

"You wouldn't recognize it from the old days," she assured him.

They talked about Los Angeles, past and present. Dorian told him about the expansion in the San Fernando Valley, and promised to show him that, too. Raif showed keen interest, but after a while she had trouble keeping her eyes open.

He finally noticed. "You're falling asleep, honey. Go to bed."

"I *am* a little tired. But I'll help you clean up the kitchen first."

"You probably don't even know where the dishwasher is," he teased.

"I do, too. I store movie cassettes in it."

"That wouldn't surprise me." He turned her around and swatted her lightly on the bottom. "Stop arguing and get into bed."

Dorian opened the draperies in the bedroom so they could gaze out at the view, then removed her filmy robe and slid gratefully between the cool sheets. The faint domestic sounds from the kitchen filled her with joy. Raif seemed completely at home in her surroundings. Everything was working out perfectly.

She was fast asleep when he came in a short time later. Raif undressed quietly and slipped into bed next to her. She sighed blissfully, but didn't waken when he took her gently in his arms.

His expression was inscrutable as he stared at her delicate features in the darkness. A long time passed before Raif fell asleep.

Dorian awoke first the next morning. Raif had his face buried in the crook of her neck to avoid the rays of sunshine streaming in the window. She stroked his hair tenderly, filled with the wonder of having him there.

His lashes tickled her neck as he opened his eyes. "Good morning, angel." He raised his head to look at her. "Did you sleep well?"

"Like a log," she said ruefully. "I'm sorry I faded out on you last night."

"It was understandable. You had a strenuous evening."

She put her arms around his neck. "I'm all rested now."

His eyes darkened as he curved a hand around her breast. "Be careful. You don't know how enticing you are. We might not get out of bed all day."

"I wouldn't mind," she murmured.

His expression altered subtly. "Is that why you lured me here, woman?"

"Now you know my secret." She trailed her fingers over his thigh.

He captured her hand and kissed the palm before rolling away and getting out of bed. "I'm not that easy. First you have to show me the sights, like you promised."

Dorian was surprised, but she masked her disappointment under a joking tone. "Okay, but don't think I've given up. I'll wear down your resistance sooner or later."

Raif showered in the guest bath, then toweled himself dry with unnecessary force. He paused after plugging in his electric razor, staring at himself in the mirror.

"When are you going to stop acting like a horse's rump?" he muttered. "Why can't you compromise and be happy?" His stern reflection didn't hold any answer.

They drove down Wilshire Boulevard to downtown Los Angeles, past the art deco Bullocks Wilshire Building and the ancient, but still stately Ambassador Hotel. Yet when they reached downtown, nothing was familiar to Raif. He marveled at the modern skyscrapers, the elegant music center and posh hotels.

"I wouldn't have believed it," he stated.

"Everyone is impressed," Dorian said. "Now I'll show you the valley. You'll be amazed at how that's grown."

Instead of taking the freeway, she drove over Coldwater Canyon. The mountainous road was still bordered by beautiful homes, but the San Fernando Valley on the other side had sprawled out to almost limitless dimensions.

Raif was fascinated by the housing developments and shopping centers. They stopped several times so he could go through model homes and inspect the layout of various malls. It was early afternoon before he was finally satisfied.

"If you've had enough sightseeing, how would you like to play a little tennis?" Dorian asked.

"I could use the exercise, but I don't have a racket."

"The pro shop can loan you one. I belong to the Meadowwood Country Club."

Raif's eyebrows climbed. "That's a very prestigious club."

Dorian grinned. "Hardly. They took me in, didn't they?"

"That proves my point," he answered.

* * *

The Meadowwood Country Club had double iron gates that opened to a winding driveway ending at a colonial-style clubhouse. Beyond a broad terrace at the rear, a swimming pool overlooked an emerald-green golf course.

Lithe people with the requisite California tan lounged by the pool or played tennis on the adjoining fenced-in courts. Threading their way through the sunbathers, white-coated attendants scurried back and forth serving tall iced drinks.

"Not too shabby," Raif commented, surveying the scene. "I could get used to living like this."

"I never suspected you were a yuppie at heart," Dorian teased.

"Hey, I'm flexible." He put an arm around her shoulders. "Now we'll see if I remember how to play tennis."

Raif was slightly rusty, but his physical coordination was superb. Dorian managed to hold her own, but she was panting by the time they finished the last set.

"That was a great workout," Raif remarked as they walked off the court. "My muscles are all loosened up."

"Mine are screaming for mercy," Dorian groaned. "Let's go lie by the pool and have something tall and cold to drink."

"That's the best offer I've had all day." When she gazed at him with an arched eyebrow, he chuckled. "Well, the second best offer, anyway."

They stretched out on padded chaises with frosty glasses of iced tea, idly discussing plans for the evening.

"Do you want to have dinner after the theater or before?" Dorian asked.

"Whichever you prefer."

"You're very easy to get along with." She smiled.

"I aim to—" Raif paused as he reached up suddenly to catch a beach ball that was headed straight for him. It had gotten away from one of the youngsters playing catch in the shallow end of the pool.

"Thanks, mister," the boy called when Raif threw the ball back to him.

"Cute kid," Raif remarked with a smile.

Dorian gazed pensively at the boy's animated face. "Our child would have been about his age."

Raif's hand gripped hers. "Don't torture yourself, darling."

"I'm not. I can talk about it now."

"Are you sure you want to?" he asked quietly.

"I think we should, Raif. I realize now that I acted irrationally. Nobody was to blame. The doctor told me these things sometimes happen to perfectly healthy women. They don't know why."

"That doesn't help when you're the one who suffers the loss," he said somberly.

"But mature people handle it. You were right about me. I was too young for marriage."

"That was my fault." His hand tightened almost painfully. "I wanted you so much that I convinced myself it would work."

She shook her head. "You couldn't have talked me out of it."

"I don't agree. I was four years older. But for what it's worth, I'm sorry...for everything."

"It wasn't all bad," she said wistfully.

They gazed at each other as memories surfaced: wild, sweet memories of the past. The deep longing that surged through Dorian was mirrored in Raif's eyes.

"Let's go home," he murmured.

They walked down the hall to the bedroom in silence, but every nerve ending in Dorian's body was clamoring loudly. She stood motionless while Raif closed the drapes, bringing an intimate twilight to the room. When he walked slowly back to her, his eyes seemed incandescent in the dimness.

"Lovely Dorian." He cupped his hand around the back of her neck. "Do you have any idea how much I want to make love to you?"

"As much as I wanted you this morning?" She began to unbutton his shirt. "Or couldn't you tell?"

"I've been the world's biggest idiot! But that's all over now. I promise you."

Dorian laughed softly. "It wasn't that big a deal. I knew you'd get your priorities straight."

"I think I finally have. You're the one who gives my life meaning."

He took her in his arms and kissed her, gently at first, then with increasing ardor. His hands roamed over her back restlessly from her shoulders to her hips.

Dorian caressed his body in the same way, tracing the long triangle of his torso down to his narrow waist. After pulling his shirt out of his slacks, she ran her palms over his smooth, warm skin.

"I love the way you feel." She sighed.

He kissed her closed eyelids. "My sweet, passionate Dorian. You're enough to drive any man out of his mind."

"I've never seen you lose control." Her mouth curved in a smile as she slid his zipper down and delved into the hidden region below.

Raif drew in his breath sharply and grabbed for her hand. "You're about to," he said in a strangled voice.

"Let me touch you," she pleaded, pushing him onto the bed.

His body was rigid as he fought for control while she eased his clothes off. But when he was completely nude and she strung a line of fiery kisses over his taut stomach, Raif uttered a hoarse cry.

He rolled over, pinning her beneath him. While his mouth plundered hers with almost savage desire, he made her unmistakably aware of his aching urgency.

Dorian's excitement rose to match Raif's when he removed her clothing with frantic haste. Her passion mounted to the level of his as he returned her arousing caresses.

Their need was too great to be postponed. In a matter of moments their bodies joined and danced to a wild rhythm. The music swelled to a crescendo then slowed to a quiet beat.

After a long period of shared contentment, Raif kissed Dorian's temple. "Did I ever tell you that you're fantastic?"

"Maybe, but I wouldn't mind hearing it again."

"You will. I'm going to repeat it every morning and twice at night."

Dorian's heartbeat quickened, but she kept her voice light. "I might be spoiled by the time the weekend is over."

"I hope it won't ever end."

She turned her head for a searching look at his face. "You mean, the memory will linger on?"

"I'm asking you to marry me," he answered quietly.

"Oh, Raif, I can't believe it!" She sat up abruptly and wrapped her arms around her trembling body.

He sat up to face her. "You must know how I feel about you, sweetheart. There's never been anyone else for me."

"Or me," she answered softly.

"That proves we belong together. And this time we're mature enough to work out our problems."

Dorian gazed at him with stars in her eyes. "What problems?"

"Well, there's your business here in L.A. I would never ask you to give it up, but I don't want a long-distance marriage, either."

"Of course not! You can move in here with me."

"It's not quite that simple." Raif seemed suddenly uncomfortable.

Dorian realized he was thinking of the differences in their finances. She had to be very careful this time to preserve his pride.

"I really need you here, darling," she began cautiously. "I don't have anyone to discuss my problems with. I need you to advise me."

"I told you I'd be happy to go over your books."

"Well, that wasn't exactly what I had in mind."

Raif's eyes narrowed. "What exactly *did* you have in mind?"

"You could help me make decisions," she answered vaguely.

"Without having any idea of the shape your company is in?"

"Not financial decisions. More…uh…opinions about things."

"Like what kind of plants to put in your office?" he asked sarcastically.

She was starting to get impatient. "Why are you making an issue of this now?"

"Can you think of a better time? You expect me to drop everything and move in with you, not as an equal partner, but some kind of house pet!"

"You're asking me to make you a partner in my firm?"

"I didn't say that. I'm talking about sharing our lives as equals."

Dorian's rosy glow was dissipating fast as little nagging things began to form an ugly picture. Raif had asked questions about the financial workings of her agency almost from their first meeting in Summerville. He also told her he was impressed with her apartment and all the other trappings of her success. He even came right out and said he could get used to living this way.

"Why did you ask me to marry you, Raif?" she asked evenly.

"I'm sure you know the answer to that."

"But why tonight? Why not in Summerville? We had some very frantic interludes there, too, yet every time I tried to talk about our future together, you shied away."

"From the moment I saw you again, I knew it wasn't over. But I was afraid physical attraction wasn't enough," he answered honestly. "For either of us."

"Yet now it is." Her voice was flat.

"No! That's *not* all there is. I found that out."

"If we're talking about true love, why are you making conditions before you'll move here? You have no compelling reasons to keep you in Summerville."

"It bothers you to think I'm a failure, doesn't it, Dorian?" Raif asked slowly.

"I never said that."

"You didn't have to. Your attitude says it all." His face was stony. "You're annoyed right now because I'm giving you a hard time instead of counting my blessings. After all, you're willing to support me—as long as I perform on demand, and stay out of your business."

His contemptuous accusation stung deeply, along with his cold, hard stare. Where was all the love and tenderness he'd shown only minutes ago? Or was this the real Raif? She lashed back out of pain, wanting to hurt him as he was hurting her.

"It's a little late to start pretending you don't care about material things. That pose would be more believable if you'd proposed in Summerville before you checked out my assets.''

Raif got out of bed and pulled on his shorts. ''I hope they make you happy.'' His voice held only weariness. ''God knows I never could.''

Tears clogged Dorian's throat as she watched Raif dress. She swallowed hard and asked, ''Where are you going?''

''Does it matter?''

''I guess not,'' she whispered.

Raif paused at the door. In the darkened room his expression was unreadable. Even his voice was muted. ''Have a good life, Dorian.''

When she blinked back the tears, he was gone.

Chapter Eleven

Dorian never knew how she managed to get through that weekend. Sunday passed in a blur of pain. Raif was gone, but his presence was everywhere. The bedroom was a constant reminder, and she couldn't bear to go into the kitchen. Even the guest room bore his imprint.

How had their relationship gone so wrong, so quickly? Why hadn't she given him the partnership he wanted? She'd never cared about the money, only the sense of achievement mattered to her. If she'd given him what he wanted, he wouldn't have walked out on her.

A dozen times that weekend Dorian was tempted to phone him, to say their differences weren't irreconcilable. Yet she knew they were. Raif didn't really love her. To his credit, he'd never once said so, but without love, their marriage had no chance.

* * *

Dorian was in her office on Monday morning long before anyone else. A second sleepless night had left her impatient for dawn. She was plowing doggedly through the mound of backed-up paperwork when Karen put in an appearance.

"Well, you're an early bird," her assistant remarked. "I didn't expect you before noon at the earliest."

"I've taken too much time off already," Dorian answered tersely. "I can't believe how things have piled up."

"I handled everything I could," Karen said defensively. "The things on your desk are matters that need your personal attention."

"I realize that. I didn't mean to sound critical." Dorian massaged her temples.

Karen accepted the apology. "You look really beat. Big weekend?" she asked casually.

"More or less."

"How did the cocktail party go?"

"It was a huge success. I really appreciate all your hard work, Karen."

"No problem. Did your friend enjoy the party?" Karen asked innocently.

"Raif?" Dorian became very interested in the papers on her desk. "I suppose so."

"He's a real hunk. You don't see many guys who have it all."

"There are several letters here that have to go out immediately," Dorian said without looking up. "And tell Walter I'd like to see him in my office when he has a minute."

"Right." Karen hesitated, gazing at her employer's remote face. "Will it be business as usual this week? Shall I schedule appointments for you?"

"Of course. Why would you think otherwise?"

"Well, since your friend is visiting from Summerville, I thought..."

"My friend has gone home."

"Oh. I'm sorry," Karen murmured.

"Join the club," Dorian answered ironically.

The days merged together in a familiar pattern. Dorian went to work early and stayed late. Only the nights were different. She came home exhausted and fell into bed, but the blessed oblivion of sleep lasted for just a few hours, and even those hours were fitful. Dreams tormented her, and she awoke with tears streaming down her face. The rest of the night she paced the floor, telling herself this was only a temporary condition.

"I got over him before, and I can do it again," she muttered fiercely, even while wondering if that were remotely possible.

Toward the end of the week, a phone call threw Dorian into turmoil all over again. She was working in her private office when Karen buzzed her on the intercom to say she had a call from Summerville.

Dorian's heart started to race alarmingly. Her mouth went dry, and her fingers were icy. This was the most important conversation she would ever have. What she and Raif said to each other would decide the rest of their lives.

As she reached for the phone, Karen said, "It's a Mr. Saputo. He's calling about your house."

The disappointment was so crushing that Dorian felt numb. She sat motionless as the world turned gray and cheerless again. Finally she forced herself to pick up the receiver.

"I've got good news for you, Miss Merrill." John Saputo's voice was as professionally upbeat as ever. "The

Bronwyns came up with a new offer that I think you're going to like. This one is fair to everybody."

"What is it?" Dorian asked listlessly.

After naming the figure, he said, "I strongly urge you to take it because this is their final bid. You won't get another one like it in a hurry."

"I suppose you're right," she answered indifferently.

"I guarantee it. This is a nice little deal all around. They've already qualified for financing, and they want to take immediate possession. You won't have to worry about what's happening to your property while you're not here."

Her last tie to Summerville was about to be cut. That was the best thing that could happen, under the circumstances, but the finality was painful—like everything else in her life.

"So, can I tell the Bronwyns they've bought themselves a house?" he asked.

"Yes." She sighed.

"Splendid! Now all we have to do is get the paperwork out of the way. If you'll tell me what day you can arrange to be in my office, I'll have everything ready for you to sign."

Dorian's lethargy vanished. "Why do I have to come there? Can't you send me the papers?"

"It would save a lot of time and trouble if we finalized the deal here. Several documents have to be notarized, and we can do that right in the office."

"I can have the same thing done here at my bank. It isn't convenient for me to come back to Summerville," Dorian said tautly. The very thought panicked her.

"Well, I guess I could mail you the papers," he replied reluctantly.

"Fine. Do that."

"What about the things in the house?"

"You said the Bronwyns wanted to buy the furnishings."

"They do. I was referring to the items you excluded from the contract. The personal possessions that don't go with the house."

"I forgot about those," she muttered.

"I guess I could send them to you," he offered, anxious to seem cooperative. "But I wouldn't want to be responsible if you have anything valuable in those boxes."

Dorian violently rejected the idea of returning to Summerville, but how could she risk the loss of priceless mementos? Nothing was packed for shipping. She'd simply wrapped the fragile items in tissue paper, intending to transport the cartons in her car.

"I guess I'll have to come back, after all," she said slowly.

"That really would make things easier all around. When can I expect you?"

Dorian made up her mind swiftly. As long as there was no other way, she wanted to get the whole traumatic business over with. "I'll be there tomorrow."

The real estate agent laughed. "You really move fast once your mind is made up. Can we make the appointment for the afternoon? I have a lot of documents to draw up."

Dorian pulled up in front of her house in Summerville the next day, feeling as if she had entered a time warp. On the surface everything looked the same as it had when she'd arrived the first time. The weather was unchanged, and the quiet, tree-lined street was as peaceful as always. How could she have guessed at the torment and disillusionment that awaited her?

As though history were repeating itself, Sally leaned out of her window across the street and waved. "Welcome back," she called. "I'll be right over."

Dorian waited stoically for her friend. She had hoped to avoid seeing Sally, but that was too much to expect. As the other woman joined her, Dorian mustered a smile.

"It was such a nice surprise to look out the window and see your car," Sally exclaimed.

"What are you going to do after the baby comes? You won't have time to police the neighborhood," Dorian joked.

"It's the only way I find out anything. *You* certainly don't tell me. I didn't even know when you were coming back."

"I didn't expect to." Dorian turned away to unlock the front door. "John Saputo phoned yesterday with an acceptable offer on the house. I'll just be here long enough to sign the papers."

Sally followed her inside. "Everything certainly happened fast. Does Raif know you sold the house?"

"I'm sure he'll hear about it," Dorian answered evasively.

"Aren't you going to tell him yourself?"

This was exactly what Dorian had wanted to avoid, a discussion of her private life. She walked into the living room, tossed her purse on the couch and removed her jacket.

"I'd love to visit with you, Sally, but I have a million things to do around here before my meeting this afternoon at the real estate office."

Sally didn't take the hint. "Why don't you want to tell Raif about the house?" she persisted.

Dorian's nerves threatened to snap. "I'm sorry if this sounds rude, but I really don't have time for company right now."

The extent of Dorian's stress finally registered. "Can I stay if I promise not to ask what happened between you and Raif?" Sally asked in a subdued voice.

"We both realize you could never keep that promise." Dorian sighed.

"I know you think I'm a busybody, but I honestly care about you, Dorrie. I had such high hopes for you and Raif. You seemed so happy together before you left for Los Angeles."

"We were for a while. Raif can be very charming when he wants to be, but I discovered I never really knew him." Dorian's eyes were bleak.

"None of us did. We were all stunned when we found out."

"About what?"

"We didn't have the faintest idea he was so rich. I mean, how could anyone guess? He drives that old truck and lives so simply. We all figured he was having a hard time."

A cold chill traveled up Dorian's spine. "Why do you think Raif is rich?"

"Kenny says Raif is so loaded he could retire if he wanted to."

"That doesn't answer my question. Where did you get your information?" Dorian asked sharply.

"Everybody found out when Raif bought that tract of land next to Barnaby's. He plans to build a whole development of moderate-priced homes on it."

"What makes you think he has the necessary capital? That's the property he was trying to get Barnaby interested in the night we all had dinner at his house. Barnaby must be financing the deal."

"No, it's Raif's company," Sally insisted. "He hired Barnaby as supervisor. But the best news of all is Raif made Kenny foreman of the entire job. Isn't that fantastic? Our money worries are finally over."

At any other time Dorian would have been delighted for her friends. Now, she barely heard Sally out. "Where would Raif raise the cash he'd need for a project that big?"

"It was like pulling teeth to get the story out of him. You know how Raif hates to talk about himself, although I can't imagine why. You wouldn't believe the things that man is involved in."

Dorian gritted her teeth. "Will you kindly tell me?"

"I do tend to run on, don't I?" Sally laughed. "Well, anyway, after working on a big government housing project somewhere overseas, Raif went to South America and formed his own construction company. They have a lot of undeveloped land down there, and his crews hacked away acres of jungle and built houses. It must have been very exciting, but he doesn't like to talk about it."

Dorian was struggling to adjust to this new concept of Raif. "What reason would he have for keeping all of this a secret?" she asked helplessly.

"The land he cleared was part of a rain forest. That was before anyone knew the effect it would have on the ecology, but he feels a lot of regret."

Dorian suddenly remembered Raif's concern for the environment. "He used to lecture me about people poisoning the atmosphere and the necessity for recycling," she said slowly.

"He's dead serious about it. Raif has been lobbying to get a bill through congress on the conservation issue. He flew to Washington to testify a couple of weeks ago."

"Was that while I was here?" Dorian asked.

"I guess it must have been."

Everything was starting to fall into place for Dorian. Raif's mysterious absence when she thought he was with Linda. The enigmatic phone call the night she had dinner alone with him at his house.

"Raif is a really compassionate person," Sally said. "He's made a difference in a lot of people's lives."

"Yes, he has." Dorian's reply was almost inaudible.

"If you know that, don't make the same mistake you made before," Sally implored.

"You don't understand," Dorian answered hopelessly.

"I can see you're both still in love with each other, no matter how often you deny it."

Dorian could have told her she was half-right. Even when she'd felt Raif was only using her, she couldn't stop loving him. The realization that she'd thrown away her chance for happiness was almost more than Dorian could bear.

"Talk to him before you leave," Sally coaxed. "You got to be friends again while you were here. At least stay in touch."

"I'll think about it," Dorian murmured.

"Do more than think," Sally urged. "You'll never find another man like Raif."

Dorian was reaching the limit of endurance. "I have a lot to do, Sally, and I don't have much time."

"Okay, I'll leave you alone. But don't drop out of our lives. Friends are too precious."

After Sally left, Dorian sank down on the couch as the enormity of her misconception began to sink in. Raif had asked her to marry him out of love, and she'd answered with the worst kind of accusations. Once again she'd questioned his love, but this time her mistake was irreversible. Raif would never forgive her for the things she'd said.

Misery enfolded Dorian like a shroud, but her punishment wasn't complete yet. One more trial lay ahead, perhaps the most difficult one of her life. She had to apologize to Raif. It wouldn't atone for her sins, but he deserved to hear her admit them.

Raif wasn't home. When his answering machine clicked on and she heard his voice, Dorian's heart began to pound. She listened to the entire taped instructions, even though she didn't intend to leave a message. That would be the cowardly way out.

She cradled the receiver finally, wondering what to do next. Raif could be anywhere. Carrie or Barnaby might be able to tell her, but she didn't want to speak to either of them. It would involve preliminary small talk that Dorian didn't feel capable of. After no other solution occurred to her, she reluctantly phoned Carrie at the Center.

The older woman was very cordial. At least Raif hadn't confided in her. Not that he was likely to, but it would have been terribly awkward.

"How nice to hear from you, Dorian," Carrie said. "I asked Raif when you were returning, but he said he didn't know."

"That's why I'm calling." Dorian got right to the point. "Do you know where I can find him?"

"You're in luck. He just dropped by a few minutes ago. I'll get him for you."

Dorian's hands were clammy as she waited for what seemed like a long time. Was Raif refusing to talk to her? That would be the ultimate rebuke. When he finally came on the line, her knuckles were white from clenching the phone.

"Dorian?" Raif's voice was coolly polite. "Carrie said you wanted to speak to me."

The solid wall of his indifference inhibited her. "Yes, I do," was all she could manage.

When she didn't elaborate, he asked with restrained impatience, "Could you tell me what it is? I'm rather busy at the moment."

"What I have to say will take a little time. Could we meet someplace?"

"I'm afraid that's impossible," he answered adamantly.

This was turning into a nightmare, but Dorian forced herself to persevere. "Please, Raif. I won't keep you long, I promise, but I have to talk to you."

The desperation in her voice swayed him, but only a little. "What's the point, Dorian? We said everything we have to say to each other."

"I don't blame you for being angry," she said haltingly.

"I'll admit I was at the time, but I'm not any longer. Let's just say you were right about everything and forget the whole incident."

"I can't forget it. I haven't thought about anything else all week. That's what I want to talk to you about."

"Are you prepared to offer a compromise?" he asked mockingly. "Maybe a full partnership *was* too much to expect. My qualifications are in a less cerebral field. Were you thinking of making me vice president in charge of paper clips?"

"I guess I deserve that," she said faintly.

"Damn it, Dorian! Don't try to make me feel guilty."

"Why should you? You have every right to feel the way you do. I'm only sorry you won't meet with me one last time."

"What purpose would it serve?" He sounded almost plaintive. "We only hurt each other when we're together."

She took heart from his inadvertent admission that he'd been hurt, too. It showed a small chink in his armor against her.

"Please give me just fifteen minutes, Raif. I'll meet you wherever you say." She could hardly breathe as the silence at his end deepened.

Finally he said, "Okay. I'll meet you at the Metropole Coffee Shop in half an hour."

Dorian was already seated at a table when Raif entered the restaurant. As he approached she drank in every detail of his lithe body and rugged face, knowing this was her last glimpse.

Raif pulled out the chair opposite her without any show of emotion. He could have been joining a total stranger. "Have you been waiting long?" he asked with conventional courtesy.

"No, I just got here," she lied.

"Would you care for something to eat?"

"No thanks, I won't keep you that long."

"You can order something. I'm not in that big a rush."

"I really don't want anything." This sparring was painful for both of them, but now that he was here, Dorian didn't know how to begin. Finally she took a deep breath and plunged in. "Thank you for coming, Raif."

His mouth curled sardonically. "Did I have a choice? You're used to getting your own way. What is it you want this time, Dorian?"

"Only to apologize for misjudging you."

"What makes you think you did?"

"I accused you unjustly. I don't know how I could have said such terrible things."

"That's easy," he answered tersely. "Because you believed them."

"Maybe at the time, but you would have wondered, too, if our situations were reversed. I kept hoping all those nights we spent together here in Summerville meant more to you than just great sex. I waited for you to ask me to marry you, or simply to say you loved me. But you never did. Even in Los Angeles you never said those three words. All you talked about was how you could help me be more successful."

"How about you, Dorian? What did you want from *me* beyond satisfying sex? We were equals while I made love to you, but when we got out of bed you regarded me as a failure."

"That's not true!"

"Isn't it? Then why were you always trying to make me over in your image?"

"I thought you'd messed up somehow. I wanted to help you pick up the pieces."

Raif's taut body suddenly relaxed, and he leaned back in his chair. "We could continue to hurl accusations and defend ourselves against them, but it wouldn't change anything. I always felt the breakup of our marriage was a tragic misunderstanding. Now I realize it was inevitable. Our mistake was in trying to resurrect a loving relationship that never existed."

Every word cut into Dorian like a knife. Raif was admitting he never loved her. It would be useless to tell him she'd never *stopped* loving him. His dispassionate calm told her as much as his words, that it was over between them. All that remained was to say goodbye.

She raised her chin gallantly. "You may not believe this, but I was happy to hear you've fulfilled your ambitions. Goodbye and good luck, Raif."

"Wait a minute." His eyes narrowed. "What did you hear about me?"

"Sally told me about your success in South America, and the project you're planning here in Summerville."

"So that's why you decided I wasn't interested in taking over your business." Raif's expression hardened. "I thought you'd given me the benefit of the doubt when you cooled off. But that wasn't it, was it, Dorian? Suddenly I became an attractive prospect again. That's the reason you insisted on this meeting, isn't it?"

"How could you even think such a thing?"

"You taught me to be suspicious of people's motives," he answered derisively. "Before you came back into my life I was a very open guy."

"Oh, really? Is that why you pretended to be down on your luck when we met again after so many years?"

"That was your assumption. I never pleaded poverty."

"You knew I'd gotten that impression, but you did nothing to correct it."

"Rightly so, as it turned out," he said dryly. "Besides, you were having such a good time feeling superior to me that I didn't want to spoil your fun."

"Did it ever occur to you that I was only trying to win your approval?" she demanded. "To show you I'd finally grown up?"

Raif's mocking smile vanished. "That was the whole trouble with us. We led separate lives emotionally."

"You never shared *anything* with me, not even the work you're doing for conservation."

"I tried to tell you. I intended to that first night we had dinner at my house, but you left without giving me a chance."

"I'll admit that was my fault. It was another misunderstanding on my part. But there were other times you could have discussed it with me."

"Every time I started to talk about the ecology, you either made a joke or changed the subject. Finally I concluded you weren't interested."

Dorian felt the same defeat Raif had felt earlier. Everything had conspired against them. "I'm sorry," she said quietly. "Add that to my other apology."

"I haven't been entirely blameless myself. We couldn't have made more mistakes if we'd tried." Raif sighed.

"I know," she answered in a muted voice.

"Well, at least we aired our grievances. Now we can get on with our lives."

"Will you be glad to go back to work?" Dorian asked.

"I can hardly wait to break ground." His remote expression warmed. "The sort of housing I plan to build is sorely needed here."

"It was kind of you to hire Ken."

"That wasn't charity. He's a good man. I'm fortunate to have him in my organization."

"How about Barnaby? He doesn't have any experience. Why did you give him a job?"

"He'll be an asset, too. Barnaby is experienced at handling people. He'll keep things running without alienating anyone. That's what makes a good supervisor."

Dorian gazed at Raif thoughtfully. "You never needed Barnaby's money. Why did you suggest he invest with you?"

"I didn't. He was the one who wanted to buy in, but I convinced him to work for me instead."

"That means Barnaby knew you were the man behind the project," Dorian said slowly.

"He insisted on getting involved. I had to tell him, but I made him promise to keep it a secret."

"From me, you mean," she said steadily.

"I intended to tell you myself, but by then you'd built up so many misconceptions about me. I was afraid you'd be angry."

"That's a safe assumption," she replied ironically.

"I was waiting for the right moment...which never presented itself," he said with the same irony.

"Well, now you don't have anything to hide anymore, and you've made a lot of people happy."

"I'm pleased that I've been able to help my friends, but this housing project has much broader consequences. If we can attract business to Summerville, the whole community will benefit."

Dorian couldn't bear to watch the way his face lit with enthusiasm when he talked about his work. Raif's life was full and rewarding. There was no place in it for her.

When he became aware of her silence, his animation died. "Forgive me for getting carried away. I'm sure none of this interests you."

"Yes it does. I'm a Summerville girl, remember?" She forced a smile.

"Not for a long time." Raif gazed dispassionately at her expensively casual hairstyle and chic outfit. "What are *your* plans for the future? Something glamorous, no doubt."

If he only knew how empty her life was without him. Raif had taken all the joy out of her days. They were as lifeless as the pages of a calendar. All she had left was her pride, and Dorian needed to preserve that.

"I'm terribly busy right now. The sale of my house ouldn't have come at a worse time. That's why I'm here, o sign the papers."

"I hadn't heard. Did you get your price?" he asked.

"Close enough. I can't wait to close the deal so I can get ack to the office."

"You work too hard." Raif scanned her face, noticing e smudges of fatigue under her eyes. "You should get ore fun out of life," he said more gently.

The last thing Dorian wanted was his pity! She hastily vented an exciting life for herself. "I *have* been working ard the last few days, but that's so I can get away for a eek. There's a wonderful convention in Paris that I've een invited to attend."

"Trust you to find a way to combine business and leasure," he remarked dryly.

"This trip will be mainly pleasure," she assured him. "I lan to spend most of my days shopping for haute couure, and my nights dancing till dawn."

"Sounds like your kind of vacation. I hope you enjoy ."

"I will." She couldn't endure his polite indifference a cond longer. Glancing at her watch she exclaimed, Goodness, look at the time. I have to run."

An awkward moment developed as they stood facing ach other. The knowledge that this was the last time they rould meet called for something special, but neither knew vhat to say.

Finally Raif extended his hand. "Goodbye, Dorian. I vish you all the best."

"You, too," she murmured.

His grip tightened for an instant, then he released her and. Dorian held her head high as she walked to the door vithout looking back. Although her heart was fracturing

into a million pieces, she accepted the fact that she'd lo
Raif forever.

Raif threw himself into work with a frenzy. He was c
the site from early morning until darkness fell, involvin
himself in everything. He supervised the temporary con
struction shacks being erected, and double-checked plan
the architect had already okayed.

"That's what you have other people to do," Ken con
plained. "I'm beginning to think you don't trust us."

"I wouldn't have hired you if I didn't," Raif replie
curtly. "I simply like to keep on top of things."

"You're going to burn out at this rate. Don't you ev
sleep?"

"Not much," Raif muttered somberly. When Ke
glanced at him with a slight frown, Raif forced a grin
"I'm always like this at the start of a project. I'll slack o
later on."

"I hope so, before you self-destruct."

Ken would have been even more concerned if he'
known how Raif spent his evenings. After a grueling da
on the job, he slumped into a chair and dozed off from
sheer exhaustion. The remainder of the night he wan
dered around the house, or simply stood at the windo
staring into the darkness.

Raif no longer cooked for himself. When he remem
bered to eat, he dropped in at the nearest coffee shop
Several days after the meeting with Dorian, he got hungr
about three in the afternoon. He'd skipped lunch, and ha
only juice and coffee for breakfast.

While his order was being prepared, Raif glanced idly a
a newspaper someone had left on the counter. Suddenly h
torpor vanished and his entire body grew taut as he read a

rticle on the front page. An airplane bound for Paris had
ashed, killing everyone on board.

"She couldn't be on that plane," he whispered through
hite lips. "Dozens of planes fly to Paris every day."

In spite of the assurance to himself, he riffled the pages
pidly. "Why the hell don't they give the names of the
assengers?" he groaned. When he couldn't find any more
formation, he started for the door.

"Where are you going, mister?" the waitress called.
Your soup will get cold." After Raif flung a bill on the
unter and raced out without answering, she showed the
ll to another waitress. "Look what the guy left, and he
dn't even eat anything. The only people who fling money
ke this around are either crazy, or in love."

"It's the same thing, honey," the other woman ad-
sed.

Dorian went through her own private hell after leaving
ummerville. Her days and nights continued to follow
uch the same pattern as Raif's. On that day, however, the
rain finally caught up with her. A pounding headache
ade work virtually impossible. She couldn't concentrate
n the simplest task.

Her assistant came into Dorian's office as she was hold-
g her head in her hands. "Is something wrong?" Karen
sked in alarm.

"Just a little headache. It's nothing."

"Nothing! You look like a flower that's been out of
ater too long."

Dorian smiled wanly. "Thanks. That makes me feel a lot
etter."

"Why don't you go home and go to bed?"

"I can't. I have an appointment with Jerry Kennicott at
vo, and an article to write for the agency newsletter, not

to mention all of this." Dorian gestured at a stack of fol
ers on her desk.

"I'll reschedule your appointment, and the rest c.
wait. You simply have to take care of yourself."

"I do feel kind of rotten," Dorian admitted.

"I'll take care of everything around here. Go home."

"Maybe I will. But tell Kennicott something une
pected came up, and tell everyone else who calls that I'
unavailable at the moment."

"It isn't a crime to be under the weather. You aren't s
perwoman," Karen scolded.

Dorian's mouth curved wryly. "I found that out a
ready, but the rest of the world doesn't have to know. Ju
do as I say."

"Okay, if you promise to turn off your phone and a
swering machine. There's no point in going home if you'
simply going to work from there."

"Don't worry. I don't want to talk to anybody."

Dorian happened to receive a high volume of calls th
day. Karen was kept busy on the telephone, juggling the
When Raif called she put him on hold originally.

He was at the breaking point when she finally came ba
on the line. "Where the hell have you been?" he storme

"I'm sorry, sir, but it's a little frantic around here t
day."

Raif's blood chilled. The news media always gathere
background material on victims of a disaster. "Is Doria
all right?" he asked urgently.

"Who is this?" Karen asked.

"What difference does it make?" Raif shouted. "Ju
tell me, is she all right?"

"Miss Merrill isn't available at the moment," Kare
answered primly.

"Where is she?"

"She's out of the office. That's all I can tell you."

Raif forced himself to ask the question. "Was she on that plane?"

"What plane?" Karen asked blankly.

"Don't play games with me, Karen! *Was she on that plane?*"

"Who is this? Do I know you?"

"It's Raif Dangerfield, and I have to know!"

"Why didn't you say so? Dorian didn't feel well so she left early, but don't tell her I—"

Raif didn't wait to hear the rest. He hung up for an instant, then dialed Dorian's number. When there was no answer after he let it ring for long minutes, he dashed out to his truck.

"Karen wouldn't lie to me," he muttered through clenched teeth. "But where is Dorian?"

Raif made the two-hour trip to Los Angeles in a little over an hour. The city traffic slowed him down, but after what seemed like an eternity, he screeched to a halt in front of Dorian's building.

At any other time the look on the doorman's face would have amused Raif, but he barely saw the man. After fuming at the slowness of the elevator, he raced down the hall and held his finger on Dorian's bell.

Agonizing minutes passed. Raif was considering breaking down the door when he heard sounds inside. The door opened and Dorian stood there, struggling to pull a robe over a blue chiffon nightgown. She looked slightly dazed, and her cheeks were rosy with sleep.

Raif stared at her as though seeing a rare piece of art. "You're alive," he breathed.

Dorian scarcely heard him. She stared back incredu
lously, extending her hand toward him tentatively. "Am
still asleep?" she whispered.

He took her in his arms, effectively answering her ques
tion. She was bruised by his rigid frame, her breathing a
most cut off by his smothering embrace, but Dorian didn
complain.

She uttered incoherent little cries of joy as Raif covere
her face and neck with frenzied kisses. He was sayin
something, but she couldn't make out the words. Not tha
they mattered. A miracle had occurred. Raif had com
back to her!

Finally he gained control of himself and held her mor
gently. "I wanted to die, too, when I thought I'd lost you."

"Too?" She drew back slightly to touch the ravage
lines in his face.

"I was afraid you were on that plane that went dow
today, the one to Paris."

Dorian suddenly realized why he was there. Naturall
he'd be upset if he thought she'd been killed. The shoc
had obviously traumatized him.

"I'm sorry you were worried," she said in a mute
voice.

"I was frantic! You never mentioned what day you wer
leaving. I finally reached Karen and she told me you wer
all right, but when you didn't answer your phone I par
icked all over again."

Dorian was having trouble comprehending. "You drov
all the way to Los Angeles after Karen told you I wa
alive?"

"I had to be sure."

"You didn't even want to see me again in Summer
ville," she said uncertainly. "You sent me away."

"It was the hardest thing I've ever done—and the stupidest. When I thought I might have lost you forever, I realized how unimportant all our misunderstandings were."

"I was so miserable," Dorian whispered. "I never expected to see you again."

"I couldn't have stayed away much longer. I can't eat, I can't sleep. All I do is think about you. Will you marry me, my love?"

She looked at him searchingly. "I've made so many mistakes. Are you sure you can forgive me, Raif? I couldn't bear to lose you again."

He framed her face in his palms and gazed deeply into her eyes. "This time will be forever. I love you, Dorian."

After his tender kiss she said rapturously, "I'll move back to Summerville. It will take a little while to wind up my affairs here, but we can have weekends together. I only wish I hadn't sold the house."

"That's part of the past, angel. Our future is much brighter."

"Will we live in your house? That's fine with me," she added quickly.

"Dear little Dorian. Do you honestly think I'd ask you to give up everything for me?"

"I want to. None of it means anything without you," she answered simply.

He kissed her with deep feeling. "You'll never know how much your offer means, but it isn't necessary. When I finish the housing project in Summerville, I'll move my company to L.A."

"You wouldn't mind?" she asked doubtfully.

"I'm looking forward to it. It will be a new challenge."

Dorian felt suddenly giddy with happiness. "A bigger one than being vice president in charge of paper clips?"

He grinned, feeling the same release from tension.
"That's your loss. I would have been a damn good one."

"I haven't found anything you *can't* do," she said softly.

"You're wrong. I can't possibly get along without *you*,"
Raif answered as he swung her into his arms and started
down the hall.

* * * * *

Silhouette Special Edition

COMING NEXT MONTH

#703 SOMEONE TO TALK TO—Marie Ferrarella
Lawyer Brendan Connery was dreading the long-overdue reunion
with his ailing father. But then nurse Shelby Tyree appeared by
Brendan's side, offering to help him heal the wounds of the past....

#704 ABOVE THE CLOUDS—Bevlyn Marshall
Renowned scientist discovers abominable snowman.... Was it genius
or madness? Laura Prescott sought to save her father's reputation;
newspaperman Steve Slater sensed a story. On their Himalayan hunt
for truth, would they find love instead?

#705 THE ICE PRINCESS—Lorraine Carroll
To DeShea Ballard, family meant pain; to Nick Couvillion, it meant a
full house and kisses on both cheeks. An orphaned nephew united
them, but could one man's fire melt an ice princess?

#706 HOME COURT ADVANTAGE—Andrea Edwards
Girls' basketball coach Jenna Lauren dropped her defenses once
boys' coach Rob Fagan came a-courting...again. Familiar hallways
harkened back to high school romance, but this time, love wasn't just
child's play....

#707 REBEL TO THE RESCUE—Kayla Daniels
Investigator Slade Marshall was supposed to discover why
Tory Clayton's French Quarter guest house lay smoldering in ashes.
Instead, he fanned the flames...of her heart.

#708 BABY, IT'S YOU—Celeste Hamilton
Policeman Andy Baskin and accountant Meg Hathaway shirked
tradition. They got married, divorced, then, ten years later, had a
child. But one tradition prevailed—everlasting love—beckoning
them home.

AVAILABLE THIS MONTH:

#697 NAVY BABY
Debbie Macomber

#698 SLOW LARKIN'S REVENGE
Christine Rimmer

#699 TOP OF THE MOUNTAIN
Mary Curtis

#700 ROMANCING RACHEL
Natalie Bishop

#701 THE MAN SHE MARRIED
Tracy Sinclair

#702 CHILD OF THE STORM
Diana Whitney